THE ANTAGONISTS: BOOK TWO

BY BURGANDI RAKOSKA

EDITORS:

Kalie Mehaffy
Belinda Wong
Ell Eggar
Mae Kelley

A Note From The Author

This book was originally written and self-published in 2015 by a sleep-deprived disabled college student. It was often written at midnight and in the earliest hours of the morning, as the times in question made for the only free-time the author had. This book was not written with the intent to create a polished and professional masterpiece, but rather, to give the disabled community some sorely-needed representation.

In the end, a book (and its subsequent sequels) that was only meant to reach a handful of readers reached thousands, shocking the sleep-deprived author. While the typos and mistakes were not unnoticed, the desire for representation outweighed the desire for perfection. The sleep-deprived author has since worked day and night to improve her writing, though I'm afraid to say that her sleeping habits have only worsened.

The author acknowledges that publishing the paperback version with the typos and mistakes she was blinded to years ago, but can clearly see today, is a controversial move. However, it is the author's belief that the mistakes are a symbol of where she started and how far she, and her readers, have come.

As always, thank you for your support.

Burgandi Rakoska

I was going to dedicate this book to you but then I found out about that embarrassing thing that you did in middle school.

PROLOGUE

January 3rd

The king was going to fall.

Minerva Banks chewed on her bottom lip as she scanned the battlefield. She glanced around for support. The woman to her left merely offered her a shrug. The man to her right opened his mouth but quickly snapped it shut. Minnie sighed as she faced the enemy. His troops significantly outnumbered hers - in fact, she had no troops left. They had all fallen in order to protect the king. In hindsight, she realized that this had been a mistake.

Minnie's heart sank as she realized that she couldn't prevent the king's fall.

"Checkmate."

Minnie groaned at Nicolas Flamel's utterance.

His eyes sparkled as he triumphantly removed her king from the chessboard.

"You did well," Nicolas gently said, "Much better than last time."

"I really hate chess," Minnie grumbled.

Victor laughed and said, "As do I."

He clapped his brother on the shoulder before sweeping the chess pieces into the cardboard box. Minnie had the feeling that he was hastily putting the game away before she could challenge Nicolas to another rematch.

"If it helps," Perry spoke up, "My husband has never been defeated by anyone."

Nicolas modestly smiled.

Minnie's reply was drowned out by a small beep. She glanced at her phone and realized that it was a notification from her news app. The headline caused her stomach to twist:

EMBELLISHING EMBEZZLEMENT:
THE QUARTET, NEW QUARTZ CITY'S ESTEEMED SUPERHERO TEAM, IS SPEAKING UP AGAINST THE EMBEZZLING SCHEME OF NEW QUARTZ GENERAL'S CEO: GREGORY KELLINGTON.
TUNE IN: CHANNEL 2

At Minnie's command, Victor turned on the television and flipped to the right channel.

Victor and Nicolas frowned as their brother walked up to a podium.

Felix Flamel cleared his throat before booming, "My fellow citizens of New Quartz City, I would like to give a statement regarding Gregory Kellington. Kellington should be ashamed of himself. Only a cold, sadistic, monster would rob from a hospital."

Minnie rolled her eyes.

She couldn't believe that she had spent a decade worshipping the so-called superhero.

She also couldn't believe that it had only been a

week and a half since her views had been completely shattered. She was now living and working with The Quartet's sworn enemy – Victor. New Quartz City saw Victor as a vile, dangerous, supervillain.

Minnie glanced over at her new partner.

Victor was juggling three chess pieces. He paused only to take a sip of peppermint tea. One of the pieces eventually hit his head. His brother and sister-in-law hid their chuckles.

What a truly a vile, dangerous, supervillain.

Yet Minnie had sincerely thought that at one point. She had subsequently made one of the biggest mistakes of her life; she had handed evidence of embezzlement over to Felix – the leader of The Quartet. She had ultimately realized that Felix was a corrupt jerk. Minnie had been forced to work with Victor, his brother, and his sister-in-law in order to gather more evidence.

Things had become even more confusing when it was revealed that they were all sixteen-hundred-year-old sorcerers who had trained under Merlin. Most of their past was still clouded in mystery. Minnie simply knew that Nicolas, Felix, and Victor were brothers. They had joined a group known as the Brotherhood of Merlin. Nicolas had met the woman who would eventually become his wife. Felix had met a group of jerks who would eventually become his 'friends'. They all showed their pride for this group with an intricate tattoo of an 'M' on their chests and a golden 'M' pin. Unfortunately, Victor had unintentionally caused the death of Merlin. A huge fight had occurred. Sides had been created. Victor, Nicolas, and Perry had been on one side. Felix and his friends had been on the other. The seven had spent sixteen-hundred-years shaping history, for better or worse. They often blended in with the historical cultural trends, hence the current disguise of superheroes and supervillains.

Minnie wished that New Quartz City could see how corrupt The Quartet really was.

Yet they had a prophecy on their side.

The age-old prophecy supposedly placed everyone who has existed or will ever exist into three categories: Protagonists, Neutrals, and Antagonists.

Felix and the other members of The Quartet were Protagonists.

Nicolas and Perry were Neutrals.

Victor was an Antagonist.

As different as the seven were, they all seemed to agree on one thing – they couldn't care less what the prophecy stated. The Quartet used their position of positive power to secretly wreak havoc. Victor defied his title by trying to secretly help as many people as possible. Nicolas and Perry did their best to assist him, remaining anything but neutral.

At least they were on Victor's side; Minnie had a feeling that they needed all of the help that they could get.

Her heart sank as Felix continued to talk about how he had taken a civilian's phone and had photographed the evidence before Victor had destroyed it. Yes. That was exactly what had happened.

"I only hope," Felix thundered, "The Quartet can bring justice."

"Justice?" Minnie repeated.

What sort of justice could corrupt jerks bring?

She was actually sort of surprised that they were throwing Gregory Kellington under the bus. Prism/Theodore had once admitted that Kellington was a good friend of theirs.

"Felix doesn't have any friends," Perry solemnly said, "He has puppets. As soon as one of those puppets misbehaves, he severs the strings."

Minnie shivered – not just at the metaphor.

She was still getting used to the fact that Perry could read minds.

"I knew that he was going to do something like this," Victor sighed, "He always does."

Nicolas and Perry nodded.

Minnie merely frowned.

They kept making it clear that Felix was a bigoted jerk who thrived in causing as much harm as possible. Yet, at the same time, Nicolas and Perry were giving Felix an Elixir of Immortality during

Victor's Christmas dinner. It didn't make sense.

Perry leaned over and whispered, "The world doesn't make sense."

January 4th

"Are you sure that you're going to be alright?"

Minnie laughed at the expression on Victor's face. Nicolas had been fussing over him for the past quarter of an hour. Victor's eye had begun to rhythmically twitch.

Perry snorted and nudged her husband.

"Alright, alright," Nicolas chuckled, "I'm just making sure."

"Flight 131 is now boarding."

The cold female voice flooded the airport.

"That's us," Perry sadly said.

The group exchanged hugs and pleasantries.

"Victor," Nicolas sternly said, "Look after her."

Minnie's cheeks became warm.

Her flush elevated as Victor said, "I will."

"Minnie," Perry quietly said, "Look after him."

Minnie grinned and said, "I will."

January 5th

An explosion shook the entire house.

Minnie gasped as she toppled out of her bed.

She pulled herself into her wheelchair and hurried into the hallway. The platform lowered her to the ground floor. Victor was quickly shutting the door to his laboratory.

"Good morning," Victor cheerfully said, "Don't go in there for a while."

"Why not?"

"It's a long story," Victor admitted, "I won't bore you with the insignificant details. I'm just glad that I was able to save this."

It was a leather bracelet that had been carefully engraved with an 'M'.

He handed it to Minnie.

"Thanks," Minnie appreciatively said.

"Put it around your wrist," Victor commanded, "Then squeeze it for three seconds."

Minnie gave a start but complied.

She gasped as the bracelet began to magically expand. The black leather crept up her arm before engulfing her entire body. Minnie uncomfortably squirmed before realizing what was happening. Her mouth fell open as the leather settled. She had her own leather suit of armor!

"This is amazing," Minnie cried, "Thanks!"

"Don't mention it," Victor replied, "You need to be prepared if you're going to help fight The Quartet. They'll take every opportunity to remind you that you're mortal."

Minnie shivered and nodded.

"Squeeze your wrist for three seconds to return to normal," Victor instructed, "It's activated by your fingerprints only. Nobody else can use it; nobody else can force you to use it."

January 9th

Minnie was freaking out.

The owners of a laundromat had recognized her.

They hadn't said much.

They had simply said that they had enjoyed the fight.

Still, it had freaked her out so much that Victor had to drag her away.

The two ducked into an alleyway.

"Are you alright?" Victor demanded, "What's wrong?"

"They recognized me," Minnie whispered.

Victor nodded and said, "We fought The Quartet here two nights ago."

"They recognized me!"

Victor paused before slowly repeating, "We fought The Quartet here two nights ago."

"Victor, they recognized me!"

"Am I having a stroke?" Victor wondered, "We fought The Quar—"

"I know that we fought The Quartet here two

nights ago," Minnie interjected, "I just didn't expect anyone to recognize me."

Her heart was thundering.

The past few weeks had been some sort of bizarre fairytale but reality was now crashing down. Felix worked hard to ensure that everyone saw The Quartet as a group of superheroes.

What if she and Victor were caught?

She and Victor discussed this for the remainder of the night.

Victor assured her that she would never be arrested. There was a longstanding pact between him and The Quartet which ensured this.

"You could essentially get away with murder," Victor teased.

Minnie stared at him for a moment before saying, "Have you—?"

"The point is," Victor interjected, "Don't worry."

Minnie was worrying.

Victor raised an eyebrow.

"I don't think that the Dean of New Quartz University is going to be content with the fact that her student is a supervillain," Minnie pointed out.

"You never know," Victor bracingly said.

Minnie laughed before continuing, "What about my parents and sisters? What about my friends and classmates? I don't want people to know..."

She trailed off.

"Wait a minute," Minnie abruptly said, "Don't supervillains have secret identities?"

"The cowardly ones do."

"Perfect," Minnie cried.

"You're not a coward."

"Sure, I am."

Victor gave her a sad smile before saying, "If you were a coward, you would run away from me as fast as you could."

"I don't run," Minnie remarked.

Victor grinned.

He ducked into the laboratory and was preoccupied for several hours, until he finally emerged triumphant.

"This will conceal your identity," Victor promised, "Try it on."

Minnie took the object before staring at him.

It was an ordinary black mask.

"It's magical," Victor explained, "Nobody will be able to recognize you; no matter how obvious it may seem."

Minnie sighed with relief and thanked him.

"You're welcome," Victor gently said, "I've also adjusted your scabbard. It will remain invisible until you tap it three times."

He handed the invisible object to Minnie. She fumbled and ultimately dropped it. Victor snorted before bending down and feeling the ground. He ultimately found it and handed it to her once more. Minnie quickly tested to ensure that it worked. It did! She grinned before fastening it to the side of her wheelchair.

"Now," Victor continued, "We just need to come up with a persona for you."

He began to pace the room.

At long last, he cried, "The Wheeler!"

"Absolutely not."

"Yes."

"No."

"Victor—"

"Yes, The Wheeler?"

"If you weren't immortal, I would personally kill you."

January 14th

THE WHEELER AND VICTOR:
NEW QUARTZ CITY'S NOTORIOUS SUPERVILLAIN DUO

Minnie spat out her instant noodles.

Her friend had just thrust the newspaper beneath her nose.

"Isn't it amazing?" Ming cried, "Someone in a wheelchair made the front page!"

Minnie took a deep breath before rasping,

"Great."

"Who do you think The Wheeler is?"

Minnie stared at her for a moment.

She opened her mouth before closing it again.

At long last, she said, "No clue."

January 16th

Minnie's knuckles were white as she held onto the hilt.

She had her other hand on her wheel. She was turning her wheelchair to avoid the blows of her enemy's sword. She slashed her own sword and was able to get a few blows in.

Unfortunately, it wasn't long before the enemy's blade was against her neck.

Minnie sighed.

Victor stopped the stopwatch and made a few notes.

"How bad?"

"You did well," Victor assuredly said, "You're improving."

Minnie threw him a skeptical glance.

"You haven't mastered the art," Victor admitted, "However, you *are* improving."

"I'm not exactly jumping for joy," Minnie wryly said.

Victor chuckled before saying, "Let's try again."

The two raised their words and commenced the duel.

"How many swords do you have, anyway?" Minnie breathlessly asked.

"Thirteen," Victor admitted, "Not including yours."

He gently nicked Minnie in the shoulder.

She hissed in frustration and swung her arm.

Victor staggered backwards to avoid her blade.

Minnie quickly used the move that he had shown her. She grabbed his wrist and twisted. The sword fell to the ground and Victor soon joined it. Minnie held out her own sword with a shaky arm. The blade was against Victor's neck.

He grinned and cried, "You're definitely improving."

Minnie beamed before saying, "I'm still not jumping for joy."

January 20ᵗʰ

Minnie was close to tears.

She had failed a test.

She hadn't studied; there had been no time.

Every second of her free-time had been spent fighting alongside Victor.

She wheeled out of her professor's office and took a few deep breaths. They had just talked about the possibility of her withdrawing from the course before it was too late.

Minnie had insisted that she would do better.

She jumped as her phone rang.

She quickly answered.

"Any particular reason your apartment is abandoned?"

Minnie recognized her younger sister's voice.

She sighed as she realized that it was only a matter of time before this call occurred.

She was just glad that it was Gabby and not Lizzie.

She took a deep breath before bracingly saying, "Hey, Gabby."

"Don't 'Hey, Gabby' me," Gabby cried, "Why is your apartment abandoned?"

"Who says that it's abandoned?"

"I do," Gabby exclaimed, "I'm looking through your window right now. It's completely abandoned. Unless all of your things magically became invisible."

'Nope,' Minnie amusedly thought, 'Just my scabbard.'

"I moved in with my friend," Minnie ultimately said.

Gabby cackled and said, "Mom and Dad are going to freak out."

Minnie had to appreciate the eighteen-year-old's priorities.

"Which is precisely why you're not going to tell them," Minnie declared, "Or else I'll tell them that *you* were the one who took the car for a joyride last summer."

There was silence on the other line.

"You talk the talk," Gabby eventually said, "Can you walk the walk?"

Minnie laughed.

It was a long-standing inside-joke.

Minnie sobered and said, "Don't tell them."

"Fine," Gabby sighed, "Hey, have you seen the newspapers?"

Minnie promptly decided that this was not a good day.

She swallowed and croaked, "What about them?"

"There's this new supervillain out there," Gabby explained, "She calls herself The Wheeler."

She called herself no such thing.

"What about her?" Minnie squeaked.

"It's just weird," Gabby slowly said, "You've been fangirling over The Quartet for years and all of a sudden, there's this chick in a wheelchair fighting them."

Minnie swallowed and croaked, "Weird."

January 22nd

"I need your help!"

Minnie and Victor spun around.

They had been walking down the street when they had heard the cry.

A random woman was trying to get their attention. She looked like the type of woman who constantly asked to speak to the manager when her fake nails were out of stock. She was standing next to a pristine minivan. Minnie spotted a family decal on the back window.

She and Victor exchanged glances.

"How can we help you?" Victor finally asked.

The woman ignored him and cried, "We just found out that my son is going to be confined to a wheelchair."

Minnie's cheeks became hot.

"And?" Victor prompted.

The woman hesitated before asking, "You wouldn't happen to have some advice on how to overcome this tragedy?"

Minnie was adamantly refusing to make eye-contact with her.

"Ma'am," Victor quietly said, "With all due respect, the death of Merlin was a tragedy. The burning of the Library of Alexandria was a tragedy. Slavery was a tragedy. Having your tea-bag rip open in the middle of the night but not realizing it until you go to take a sip and subsequently end up with a mouthful of leaves, which shocks you to the point that you let out a scream, which is so loud that you make your friend fall out of her bed is a tragedy."

Minnie grinned at the memory.

"Your son using a wheelchair," Victor continued, "That's not a tragedy."

The woman begged to differ.

She shook her head and whispered, "You don't understand! This is...this is the worst thing that could possibly happen to him..."

"Really?" Victor amusedly asked, "I would have thought that his spontaneous death would have topped the list."

Minnie let out an ugly snort.

"Are you going to help me or not?"

"Fine," Victor sighed, "Minerva, may I get into your backpack?"

She confusedly nodded.

He rummaged around for several minutes before finding what he was looking for. He snatched it and promptly walked over to the woman's van. He hummed a small tune. Minnie tried to see what he was doing but he intentionally stood in the way. He finally stepped back and proudly gestured.

Minnie threw her head back and cackled.

Victor had used her white-out to draw a wheelchair around the decal of the boy.

The woman was as red as her designer handbag.

"You two are going to hear from my lawyer!"

"Is that supposed to scare me?" Minnie lightly said, "I'm in a wheelchair. That's the worst thing that could have ever happened to me, isn't it?"

She and Victor laughed.

The woman pulled out her phone.

Victor sobered and said, "Alright, we best be on our way."

He and Minnie quickly hurried away.

"You do realize that the white-out is permanent?"

"I do."

Minnie smiled and said, "Thanks, Victor."

"You're welcome."

January 29th

"So we meet again, my ancient nemesis," Minnie quietly said.

She glared at the staircase.

She had been chasing after Felix when he had bounded up the steps.

Minnie tapped her scabbard thrice.

It appeared and she quickly pulled out her sword.

Unfortunately, Felix was too far away.

Victor raced around the corner and paused as he

took in the situation.

"Seriously," Felix cackled, "Why the hell did you make the woman in the wheelchair your sidekick?"

"You know," Minnie muttered, "I'm starting to wonder the same thing."

Victor looked shocked.

"Felix has three abled guys on his side," Minnie explained, "Christopher can create fire, Theodore is a hypnotist, and Thomas is the strongest man in the city. Meanwhile, you've got me."

"Your will to fight is greater than theirs combined," Victor insisted.

"Great," Minnie sarcastically said, "Your sidekick's superpower is the will to fight. I'm sure that'll be the perfect opponent for fire, hypnotism, and brute strength."

"Stop patronizing yourself," Victor amusedly chastised, "Help me defeat Felix."

Minnie nodded and said, "Don't worry; I'll use my all-powerful 'will to fight' to bring them down!"

"Oh no," Felix exclaimed, "Not your all-powerful 'will to fight'! How will we ever survive your all-powerful 'will to fight'? We're doomed!"

Victor was not amused.

February 2nd

"Ssshh," Victor whispered, "Ssshh..."

Minnie winced as his fingers touched the skin around her eye. Small bursts of golden light appeared each time. Minnie was trying to ignore the pain.

"Thomas has a powerful swing," Victor sympathetically said, "It's going to be swollen for a few days."

Minnie nodded.

"Does it hurt?"

She bit her lip and shook her head.

Victor wasn't buying it.

He raced away and returned with a topical cream. He carefully applied it to the skin with the promise that it would soon become numb.

"Thanks," Minnie mumbled.

She instinctively went to touch it.

"Don't touch it," Victor advised.

Minnie was able to resist for a few minutes.

She ultimately brought her hand back up.

"Don't touch it," Victor amusedly said.

Minnie begrudgingly complied.

"I'm sorry," Victor continued, "I didn't mean for you to get hurt."

Minnie shrugged and said, "I knew what I was getting myself into."

Victor stared at her for a while but didn't comment.

February 8th

Victor slid several eggs onto Minnie's plate.

She gratefully dug in. She needed her strength as she had a huge test in a few hours.

"Gregory Kellington's trial starts today," Victor declared.

Minnie swallowed a mouthful before asking, "Should I go?"

"No."

"Are you going?"

"No."

"Is The Quartet going?"

"No."

"Why not?"

Victor shrugged and said, "Superheroes and supervillains don't ever get caught up in the legal matters. We just sort of...let it be."

Minnie spent the rest of the day contemplating Victor's statement.

She ended up failing the test.

February 14th

Minnie let out a stifling yawn.

She buried her nose in her textbook and realized that she was rereading the same paragraph. At least, she thought that it was the same paragraph. Nothing was sinking in.

She tensed as she heard the front door fly open.

Minnie uneasily tapped her scabbard. It immediately became visible. Her fingers found the hilt of her sword as she carefully listened.

"It's me," Victor called.

Minnie relaxed.

"You're home early," Minnie remarked, "How was your date?"

He entered the room. Minnie immediately clamped a hand over her mouth. Victor had a bowl on top of his head. Broth was running down his face. A small piece of a carrot was perched on the end of his nose.

"Don't," Victor warned.

Minnie couldn't help it.

She ended up cracking up.

Victor ultimately joined in.

At long last, Minnie wheezed, "He dumped his soup on your head?"

"No, no," Victor corrected, "He dumped *my* soup on my head."

"What happened?"

"I just told you—"

"*Why* did he dump his soup on your head?"

Victor shrugged and merely said, "I don't think that it's going to work out between us."

Minnie continued to laugh. She doubled over and clutched her sides while Victor impatiently his foot.

"Well," Minnie finally cried, "I was about to head over to Not Your Cup Of Tea. Do you want to come along?"

"So long as you won't dump your coffee on my head."

"No promises."

February 23rd

Minnie screamed as she was thrown across the rooftop. She ended up falling from her wheelchair, unintentionally rolling until she came to the edge of the building. She gasped as it dawned on her that she was, in fact, on a forty-story building. She quickly realized that there was no time for stomach-twisting fear. She crawled back over in her wheelchair and climbed back into it. Felix had just made the worst mistake of his life.

March 1st

Not Your Cup Of Tea was booming with a grand total of six customers.

Minnie brought her cup of coffee to her lips.

"Excuse me?"

Minnie and Victor looked up.

A man clapped Victor on the shoulder and

cried, "Can I just say that you are great? I would love to feature you in my magazine."

"Okay," Victor slowly said, "Wait, why?"

"The magazine celebrates everyday citizens who take time out of their day to hang out with handicapped people."

The man took a copy of the magazine from his briefcase. The cover featured a congressman high-fiving a man in a wheelchair.

The man jerked his head towards Minnie before saying, "I always see you hanging out with her. I just think that that's so cool, you know? It's awesome!*You're* awesome."

Victor caught Minnie's eye.

"You're right," Victor finally said, "I *am* awesome."

"So...?"

"I'd love to be in your magazine."

"Excellent!"

"Can I be on the cover?"

The man blinked before saying, "I suppose."

"Build me a statue," Victor abruptly said.

"What?"

"A statue," Victor cried, "Marble will suffice but I won't say no to gold."

Minnie smiled into her coffee.

The man merely stared at Victor.

"Well, go on," Victor demanded, "Build me a

statue."

He clapped his hands twice.

"I...I'm not gonna build you a-"

"Why not?"

"You-"

"I am a god."

Victor spread his arms out to the side.

"What the hell are you-?"

"Kneel before me!"

"I-"

"Your god commands it!"

The man shook his head and snarled, "Get over yourself; you're not that special."

"That's precisely my point," Victor quietly said, "Now get out of here before I take your magazine and shove it up your-"

The man got the point.

He quickly mumbled an apology and hurried away.

Minnie burst out laughing.

Victor chuckled alongside her.

"Can you believe that?" Victor asked, "'You are so awesome for hanging out with a person with a disability.'"

Minnie continued to laugh as Victor did impressions of the man.

"For the record," Minnie warmly said, "You are pretty awesome."

Victor gave her a tender smile before saying, "Does this mean that you're going to build me a statue?"

"Don't push it."

"Your god commands it!"

He snorted as Minnie threw a sugar-packet at him.

Victor threw one at her and was hit by three in return.

Their drinks went untouched.

March 6th

Minnie's blood was boiling.

Gregory Kellington had received the minimum sentence.

He would be out in six months.

Three with good behavior.

Minnie turned off the television and took a few deep breaths.

She felt a hand on her shoulder.

Golden ropes of light wrapped around her.

"You see," Victor softly said, "This is why superheroes and supervillains don't get caught up in the legal matters."

March 13th

Minnie had never hated anyone as much as she hated Felix Flamel.

He had spent the past week intentionally sabotaging her.

Her grades were slipping, her sanity was slipping, her physical health was slipping...

Something had to give.

March 21st

Victor was worried about her.
Lizzie was worried about her.
Gabby was worried about her.
Felix enjoyed worrying her.
Minnie was slowly unraveling.
It was alright.
She could do this.

CHAPTER ONE

Minerva Banks was going to die.

Three essays, four tests, and a presentation.

All in one week.

There was no way that she was going to make it.

Minnie was currently working on the second essay.

At least, she had typed out her name, the name of the professor, and the date. Minnie determined that this was progress, even if those were the only things that she had typed in the past hour. She exasperatedly looked around, as if hoping that one of the many books in the library would leap from the shelf and provide her with the answers.

She jumped as her phone rang.

Several people shot her annoyed looks.

"Hey, Minnie," Perry cried, "Is my brother-in-law there?"

"Sorry," Minnie apologized, "I'm at the campus library."

The annoyed looks turned into glares.

Minnie wheeled into the lobby and added, "I was just reading about your husband."

"You were?"

"He's in my textbook," Minnie explained, "He's on a list of notable French figures."

She snatched it from her backpack and glanced around. The only other people in the lobby were Geology Majors, excitedly talking about how they were going to be studying diamonds today. They weren't paying any attention to Minnie. Thus, she read aloud:

Nicolas Flamel

Born: 1330

Died: 1418

"I'm a widow?" Perry amazedly asked, "Why didn't anyone tell me?"

Minnie laughed and continued:

Nicolas Flamel was a French Catholic scribe who lived in Paris, France during the fourteenth and fifteenth century. Flamel was renowned for his charitable donations to the local churches. Flamel designed his own tombstone in 1410 – eight years before his death. There are historical rumors that Nicolas Flamel dabbed in the art of alchemy.

"Now, why would anyone think that?" Perry amusedly asked.

"'Beats me," Minnie remarked, "Did he really create his own tombstone?"

Perry giggled and said, "Victor and I did it as a joke."

That sounded about right.

"Hang on," Perry continued, "Aren't you a Psych Major?"

Minnie nodded.

She flushed and verbally clarified, "Yeah."

"What do notable French figures have to do with psychology?"

"The registration office screwed up," Minnie remarked, "I'm taking all sorts of pointless classes. Maybe it's a test to see how long it takes a Psych Major to snap."

Perry chuckled.

Minnie glanced at the clock and added, "Speaking of..."

She bade Perry goodbye and quickly wheeled across the campus.

She met up with Ming and the two started talking about the results of their midterms.

Minnie's had been less than ideal.

"Are you okay?" Ming asked, "You've seemed really stressed lately."

"Yeah," Minnie sighed, "I'm f—"

She broke off as she spotted a figure next to one of the buildings. A homeless man with frazzled hair was holding out a bowl. A group of students gave him strange looks before hurrying along. The man called after them before focusing on another student.

"Minnie," Ming cried, "Are you okay?"

"I'm fine," Minnie mumbled.

She pulled her thermos of coffee from her bag and took a long sip.

"I don't get paid enough for my job," Minnie eventually said.

"What?"

"Nothing," Minnie sighed, "I'll see you in class."

"Why don't we just go there together?" Ming asked, "It starts in two minutes."

Minnie ignored her and wheeled over to the man.

"Spare change?"

"What the hell are you doing here?" Minnie hissed, "Did you blow up the house again?"

"Yes," Victor admitted, "However, that's not the reason that I'm here."

"What *is* the reason?"

"Surveillance," Victor mysteriously said.

"Can you be a bit less cryptic?"

"No."

Victor's mouth was twitching.

Minnie had neither the time nor the patience.

She wheeled away without another word. Victor whispered her name but Minnie didn't look back. She entered the large academic building, took the elevator to the second floor, and entered the large lecture hall in the nick of time. She wheeled over to the rickety table for students with disabilities. Minnie glanced around and was surprised to see that her professor hadn't arrived yet. Minnie didn't particularly care for the course itself. She knew most of the information and the assignments were redundant. Yet Dr. Gibbons was one of the most respected professors on the campus. He had been injured in the war and consequently walked with a limp. He often talked to her about the rights of people with disabilities. He was a gentle man with a voice that barely went above a whisper.

As such, the crowded lecture hall was taken aback as he entered the room and gave a booming greeting. His actions continued to be peculiar as he talked about psychological trauma.

Minnie watched as her classmates squirmed with discomfort.

A few even left the hall.

Ming was among them.

"Minerva," Professor Gibbons thundered, "Would you mind telling us the answer?"

He was effortlessly walking towards her.

Something was definitely wrong.

Minnie squinted and realized that his eyes were golden. Her heart began to race and she broke out into a sweat. It was Felix. Minnie quickly grabbed her phone from her bag.

"Uh-uh," Felix snarled, "No phones allowed."

Minnie ignored him and quickly texted Victor. She quickly put her phone away before Felix could say anything else. She was aware of the fact that all of her classmates were staring at her. She was also aware of the fact that Felix was drawing closer and closer.

Minnie tried to remain calm.

She was losing the battle.

"What's wrong, Minerva?" Felix coyly asked.

Minnie opened her mouth but no sound came out.

"You look mad," Felix taunted, "You look ready to fight."

Minnie glanced at her gawking classmates before stammering, "I...I don't want to fight, P...Professor."

"Don't you?"

He was only several feet away.

Minnie looked around before wheeling towards the nearest door.

"Where are you going, Minerva?"

"Bathroom," Minnie called back.

"I'm afraid that I cannot allow that."

"I don't give a damn what you're afraid of!"

Minnie's reply echoed throughout the entire lecture hall. Her classmates gasped and exchanged shocked glances. Minnie inwardly groaned.

Fortunately, Victor created a marvelous distraction as he crashed through the wall and landed on a poor student's desk.

The resulting chaos was fantastic!

Students ran in every direction, stopping only to snap pictures of the 'supervillain'. In the confusion, nobody thought twice about the fact that Dr. Gibbons had disappeared in lieu of the white-haired leader of The Quartet. Minnie raced out into the hallway and ducked into the custodial closet. She squeezed her bracelet and smiled as the armor encased her body. She quickly put on the mask and headed back into the lecture hall.

Only a few straggler students remained.

One of them pointed and cried, "It's The Wheeler!"

Minnie heard Victor snicker.

"Get out of here, civilians!" Felix boomed, "She may attack!"

Minnie rolled her eyes as her classmates heeded his warning.

"What the hell, Felix?" Minnie roared, "What are you doing here?"

Felix smirked and said, "I saw you wheeling across the campus and couldn't pass up the opportunity to intimidate you."

"I'm not intimidated," Minnie growled.

She tapped her scabbard three times.

It immediately became visible and she withdrew her sword.

Felix withdrew his own.

"You should be," Felix spat.

Minnie rolled her eyes and teased, "I should be afraid of you because you disguised yourself as my professor? What's next? Are you going to dress up as one of the custodians? Or the woman who makes my salad in the dining hall? Oh, I'm really intimidated."

Felix was not amused.

The lecture hall was reduced to rubble as Victor and Felix threw balls of energy at one another. Victor brought down the remainder of the crumbling wall. Felix was able to shake himself from the debris just in time to avoid a blow from Minnie's sword. Victor picked up a table and threw it. Felix ducked and the table crashed into the expensive projector screen.

Minnie flinched at the damage.

"Time-out!" Felix abruptly screeched.

He turned to his brother and said, "I can't take this fight seriously when you're dressed like a filthy bum."

"Yeah," Minnie agreed, "Why *are* you dressed like that?"

"I knew that Felix was planning on doing something with the real Richard Gibbons," Victor quietly said, "I just wasn't sure what his actual plan was. I tried to disguise myself so that I could do some surveillance."

Minnie's eyes widened.

"Where *is* the real Richard Gibbons?" Minnie demanded, "What did you do with him?"

"I didn't kill him," Felix retorted, "If that's what you're implying."

It was.

Minnie let out a small sigh of relief.

"I locked him in a classroom in the Science Hall," Felix dismissively said.

Minnie turned to Victor and cried, "Go get him."

"But—"

"I'll take care of your brother!"

Victor hesitated before reluctantly leaving.

Minnie had just enough time to turn back towards Felix and lift her sword. Felix's blade hit her own with a scraping noise that caused Minnie to shiver. Minnie was able to force his blade away before swinging her own sword. The two feverishly fought one another. Sweat rolled down Minnie's face as she evaded Felix's blows. In hindsight, this hadn't been the best idea. She and Victor had been training for months but she was still a novice swordfighter. She knew that it was only a matter of time before Felix decapitated her. As such, she was taken aback when Felix spun around and abruptly raced away. Minnie glanced around but saw nothing that would cause him to run. She wheeled into the hallway and realized that it was empty. Minnie heard a noise on the stairwell. She raced over and peered down. There was nothing there.

"Amateur."

Minnie spun around just in time for Felix to kick her in the stomach.

Minnie screamed as she tipped backwards.

She covered her face as the wheelchair toppled down the steps. Minnie could feel the bumps and bruises forming with every painful impact. After an eternity, she ended up reaching the bottom. Her wheelchair was on top of her. Her world was a sickening blur. She lifted her head but gravity coaxed it down.

The sound of her own name caused her to stir.

She could hear running footsteps.

The wheelchair was lifted off of her.

Victor's face swam into view.

"Minerva," Victor hastily said, "Are you okay?"

"Fine," Minnie grunted.

Victor sighed with relief before whispering, "Take off your disguise."

The urgency in his voice caused Minnie to immediately squeeze her wrist. The armor shrank back down into her bracelet. She quickly took off the mask. She finally tapped her scabbard so that it became invisible.

"Felix set us up," Victor continued, "Quite impressively, I might add. You'll be alright as long as you act like a student. I have about thirty seconds to get out of here before—"

"There he is!"

"Get away from her!"

Minnie winced as she heard more footsteps.

Victor sighed and mumbled, "Make that ten seconds."

"See you at home," Minnie whispered.

"What time?"

"Four-thirty."

"Meatloaf for dinner?"

"Sounds good."

Minnie watched as Victor leapt through the window at the end of the hallway. The shouts had been courtesy of The Quartet. They were descending the stairs, along with several professors and the university police.

"Don't worry, citizen," Felix boomed, "I'll help you!"

Minnie resisted rolling her eyes. She had to keep from fighting back as Felix heroically picked her up. Theodore and Thomas picked her wheelchair up.

"Expose our secret and we expose yours," Felix hissed.

Minnie murmured that she understood. She knew that they would not hesitate to ruin her life. She wasn't about to give them the opportunity.

Felix gently set her into her chair.

One of the professors snapped a photo.

She held up her phone and asked, "Would you like this?"

"I'd love it," Felix remarked.

Christopher squeezed Minnie's shoulder before

asking, "What sort of sick monster would push a disabled woman down the stairs?"

Minnie's eyes flickered towards Felix.

He was trying his best to hold back a smirk.

Minnie's skin crawled.

It was still crawling several hours later.

She skipped her final class and headed back to Victor's house. Minnie headed straight up to her private bathroom and took a long shower. She could still feel Felix's hand on her shoulder.

Minnie eventually changed into a pair of pajamas. She took the levitating platform back down to the first floor and wheeled into the living room. Victor was sitting in the recliner; his eyes fixed on the ceiling. Minnie chuckled as she realized that he was lost in thought.

She transferred to the couch and was asleep within minutes.

She only woke up when Victor called, "Are you awake?"

"Now," Minnie mumbled.

"Sorry."

"'S'alright."

Minnie sat up and let out a huge yawn.

She smiled when she realized that Victor still looked thoughtful.

"What's so funny?" Victor questioned.

"Nothing," Minnie gently said, "You always just

look like you're on the brink of discovering the purpose of the universe."

"Nah," Victor chuckled, "Just my purpose in it."

He stretched before asking, "How long were you interrogated?"

"The police wanted to see if I knew anything," Minnie wearily said, "The medics wanted to make sure that I wasn't hurt. Professor Gibbons wanted to make sure that I knew that he wasn't hurt. The Dean wanted to make sure that I wouldn't sue. Felix wanted to make sure that I was as uncomfortable as possible."

Victor looked sympathetic.

Minnie wasn't in the mood for sympathy. Her stomach churned as she thought about Felix. He was truly the worst person that Minnie had ever met.

Victor ducked into the kitchen to finish preparing the meatloaf.

The two eventually sat down for dinner.

"How exactly did Felix set you up?" Minnie questioned.

"He sent me to the Science Hall," Victor pointed out, "Apparently the Geology Majors were examining diamonds today. The cops thought that I was there to steal them."

Minnie sighed and said, "I really hate your brother."

Victor looked uncomfortable.

"At least Dr. Gibbons was alright," Victor

eventually said.

Minnie nodded.

Her phone beeped and she skimmed a new email.

She immediately groaned.

"What's wrong?"

"Thanks to Felix," Minnie muttered, "I'm no longer the President of New Quartz University's Club for Students with Disabilities."

"Why not?"

"Because there's no longer a Club for Students with Disabilities," Minnie growled, "It's going to cost $13,000 to repair the damages from today's fight. NQU is shutting down all of the low-level clubs to save money."

Victor rubbed the back of his neck and mumbled an apology.

"It's not your fault."

Minnie's tone was clipped.

Yet she meant every word.

It wasn't his fault.

It was Felix's fault.

"You don't really think about the economic consequences when you're fighting," Victor admitted, "You just do whatever you can to take down your enemy."

Minnie nodded.

Victor tried to change the subject by saying,

"Speaking of NQU, how's the football team doing this year?"

"They're terrible," Minnie chuckled, "Though the players are happy. They're getting a brand new scoreboard next week."

Victor's comment was drowned out by a large roar.

His purple eyes widened.

He screamed something incoherent.

Minnie suddenly felt as though she was being stabbed by twenty swords. She could feel the white hot blades pierce every inch of her skin. She was unaware of the fact that she was screaming. She was unaware of the fact that she was falling. She was unaware of the fact that she was no longer in the dining room. Minnie was only aware of the pain.

Something finally snapped and she was thrown into darkness.

CHAPTER TWO

Minnie's screams echoed throughout the entire room.

Her hands and knees hit the unforgiving ground. Minnie continued to scream as the blades sliced through her body. She realized that the blades weren't really there, though she couldn't find another way to describe the pain. It was the worst pain that she had ever experienced. Stinging tears blinded her vision. Her entire body lurched and twisted.

People were screaming all around her.

"WHAT HAVE YOU DONE?"

"MINERVA?"

"WHAT'S HAPPENING?"

"VICTOR, STOP!"

"WHAT'S GOING ON?"

"MINERVA!"

And then, Minnie heard a calm voice; one that drowned out the rest:

'It's okay, Minnie.'

The voice rang throughout Minnie's mind.

She immediately recognized it and subsequently found herself relaxing.

Her head was tilted backwards and a cold liquid was poured down her throat.

The pain immediately faded away and was

replaced by a welcoming numbness. Minnie's vision cleared and Perry's smiling face swam into view.

"There you are," Perry gently said, "Better?"

Minnie clumsily lurched forward and the two women embraced.

"It's alright," Perry whispered, "You're going to be alright."

Minnie pulled back. She was too weak to take in her surroundings. In fact, there was only one thing caught her gaze. Victor and Nicolas were standing several feet away. The latter was restraining the former. Victor looked outraged. Minnie guiltily stared at the floor.

"He's not mad at you," Perry whispered, "He's mad at R."

Victor was mad at a letter from the alphabet?

Minnie was too tired to think straight.

"Right now," Victor growled, "I'm mad at Nicolas. Let me GO!"

Minnie jumped at the intensity of his last word.

Nicolas didn't even flinch.

"I'm not going to attack R," Victor promised, "I just want to make sure that my friend hasn't sustained serious damage from his boneheaded move."

Nicolas apprehensively released his brother.

He was at Minnie's side in an instant.

"I'm sorry," Minnie croaked.

"Don't be," Victor immediately said, "You did nothing wrong. Other mortals have died undergoing what you just did. Only a fool would do something so risky!"

His last sentence was quite loud.

"What was it?" Minnie asked.

"It was a Summoning Spell," Victor explained, "We were essentially ripped from one part of the world and thrown into another."

Minnie dazedly nodded.

In that case, where were they thrown?

She took in her surroundings.

They were in a large stone chamber. It was quite beautiful. The windows stretched to the vaulted ceiling, from which a chandelier was hanging. Beyond the windows was a view of green grounds and an ocean. The only piece of furniture in the room was a golden chair which sat upon a stone dais. A muscular man with a square jaw was sitting in the chair. A crown sat upon his golden locks. He wore a red cloak that ended at his ankles.

The man seemed perfectly unperturbed by Minnie's disturbance. Several men and women were standing next to his chair. Minnie couldn't see what their expressions were – the hoods of their cloaks were drawn. Minnie glanced over her shoulder and saw that there were at least fifty other people in the room. They were all staring at her with a mixture of horror and sympathy.

Minnie didn't know which look was worse.

"Victor," Minnie whispered, "Who…where…?"

"This is the Brotherhood of Merlin," Victor explained, "Welcome to Castle Tintagel."

Minnie's face burned.

She had made a fool of herself in front of the Brotherhood.

"You didn't make a fool of yourself," Perry whispered, "R made a fool of himself."

"Who's R?" Minnie mumbled.

"Surely Victor has told you about me?"

The booming voice caused everyone in the room to jump.

It had come from the man on the golden chair.

He slowly stood up and everyone else dropped.

Minnie looked around in alarm. She relaxed slightly as she realized that everyone had merely dropped to their hands and knees. They were kneeling before the man. It was obvious that Nicolas, Perry, and Victor were very reluctant to do so. They were kneeling nonetheless. Minnie had already been kneeling. She shifted into a more comfortable position and looked up.

The man towered over her as he asked, "Has Victor told you about me?"

"N…no," Minnie stammered.

The man scowled before eloquently saying, "My

name is Arthur; I was once the King of Britain. I am now the King of the Brotherhood of Merlin. I am the wielder of Excalibur."

He pulled an impressive looking sword from his scabbard before continuing, "I am the one who summoned you."

"Nearly killing her in the process," Victor spoke up.

Arthur sharply turned towards him.

"Victor," Nicolas hissed.

"I was told that she was immortal," Arthur remarked, "Is this not the case?"

Victor turned to Nicolas and sarcastically said, "Am I allowed to speak?"

Nicolas exasperatedly nodded.

"Of course she's not immortal," Victor burst out, "Why the hell would you think that you son of a b—"

The rest of his sentence was drowned out by Nicolas' hand.

Arthur frowned and said, "It appears that I've been misinformed."

The Flamels and Minnie exchanged glances.

"Who told you that I was immortal?" Minnie questioned.

One of the figures on the dais slowly removed their hood.

Minnie was unable to stifle a groan.

Felix smirked at her before saying, "I deeply

apologize, King Arthur. I assumed that Victor had given her the Elixir of Life when he had given her the golden pin. My bad."

There was a commotion to Minnie's right. She looked over and saw that Victor had leapt to his feet and had attempted to charge at Felix. Unfortunately, Nicolas had rather skillfully tackled him. Victor's eyes held fire as he tried to squirm away from one brother in order to attack the other.

"Stop it," Nicolas hissed, "You know as well as I do that you walk on a thin tightrope around here. Don't fall off within the first five minutes. For God's sake, do you remember what happened the last time that you made the Brotherhood angry?"

This got Victor's attention.

He slackened and whispered an apology.

"Don't apologize to me," Nicolas sternly said.

Victor gritted his teeth and said, "I'm sorry, Your Highness."

He pushed Nicolas away and pushed himself back onto his knees.

Nicolas did the same.

Arthur surveyed Victor for a moment before calmly saying, "I accept your apology. After all, I know how it feels when a friend is injured due to the carelessness of another."

Minnie could practically feel the heat coming out of Victor's eyes.

She reached over and comfortingly squeezed his shoulder. In doing so, the rope of mysterious golden light swirled around their arms. It quickly faded away but it wasn't quick enough. Nicolas and Perry exchanged fearful glances.

"All rise," Arthur softly said.

Minnie climbed back into her wheelchair.

Everyone else stood up.

Arthur slowly walked over to Victor.

For a moment, it looked as though he was sizing Victor up.

All at once, he swung and punched Victor in the jaw.

Victor reeled back and collapsed.

Minnie and Perry cried his name.

"Hey, HEY!" Nicolas roared.

He leapt between Arthur and his brother.

Arthur pushed him aside and bellowed, "I SUMMONED YOU HERE TODAY BECAUSE I FEARED THE WORST! AND NOW, YOU HAVE PROVEN THAT MY FEARS WERE CORRECT! ARE YOU A FOOL, VICTOR FLAMEL?"

Victor grunted an incoherent response.

Perry crouched down and inspected his jaw.

"DO YOU REMEMBER WHAT HAPPENED THE LAST TIME?" Arthur roared.

"Of course I do," Victor spat, "Felix won't let me forget."

"NOR SHOULD YOU," Arthur shouted, "YOU COLOSSAL IDIOT!"

He kicked Victor in the stomach.

"Stop it," Minnie shrieked, "Leave him alone!"

She reached for her scabbard but Nicolas hastily grabbed her arm.

He leaned over and whispered, "That's the last thing that you want to do."

Minnie hesitated before nodding.

Nicolas straightened up and sharply said, "Your Highness, this is nothing more than a simple misunderstanding."

Arthur raised his eyebrows.

"We know what you're thinking," Perry added, "But it's not like that."

Minnie begged to differ.

She had no idea what Arthur was thinking.

She confusedly glanced back and forth between the Flamels and Arthur.

"Do you expect me to believe that?" Arthur demanded.

"It's true," Victor retorted, "Minerva and I are just friends."

Minnie blinked and cried, "Is that what this is all about?"

"That and then some," Nicolas muttered.

Arthur turned towards Minnie.

"Like Victor said," Minnie firmly said, "We're just

friends."

Arthur merely rolled his eyes and turned back towards Victor.

He seized the front of Victor's shirt and pulled him to his feet.

"Give me one good reason why I shouldn't kill you," Arthur demanded.

Minnie shivered at the malice his tone.

Oddly enough, a twisted smile formed on Victor's face.

"Because," Victor simply said, "You hate the thought of my brother succeeding more than you hate the thought of me failing."

Arthur didn't deny it.

Nevertheless, Victor's statement didn't quench his anger. On the contrary, Arthur feverishly threw Victor into Nicolas. The two brothers straightened up and glared at him.

The sound of sharp heels against a stone floor caused the group to turn.

A woman was walking through the crowd.

Or rather, the crowd was leaping aside so that the woman could walk.

Minnie could immediately see why. She was the most beautiful woman that Minnie had ever seen. Her skin was slightly darker than Minnie's. She had a tattoo on her neck of an ace card with an arrow plunging through it. Her hair was light blonde and her makeup was on point. She wore a black dress with a slit that ran up her leg.

Minnie realized that Victor, Nicolas, and Perry were all smiling.

The woman spoke in a sultry voice, "So sorry to interrupt, R. I just wanted to make sure that my friends were okay."

"Miss Kiss," Victor reverentially said, "I was wondering where you were hiding."

Miss Kiss smiled and said, "Oh, I don't hide."

"Minnie," Perry proudly said, "This is Misrak Kissinger – a good friend of ours."

"One of the few that we have left in this castle," Victor muttered.

"'Not true," Miss Kiss remarked, "You have a lot of friends here. They're just cowards."

Sure enough, Minnie noticed that most of the Brotherhood was squirming. It was clear that they had disapproved of Arthur's abuse. Yet nobody had wanted to speak up.

Miss Kiss was the exception.

"Now, R," Miss Kiss sweetly said, "This is important, darling, so listen closely. We all know what Victor once did. Do you honestly think that a moment has gone by when it hasn't tugged on the back of his mind? Not to mention that you and Felix are constantly bringing it up."

She stepped closer to Arthur and continued,

"But what you two have always failed to see is that Victor Flamel is a damned good man. He made a mistake once and he has spent every day of his life trying to repent."

"What is your point?" Arthur snapped.

"I know that you hate him," Miss Kiss declared, "But do you honestly think that Victor would be foolish enough to repeat history? Furthermore, do you honestly think that Nicky and Perry are foolish enough to let him?"

Even Arthur couldn't admit that.

Yet Minnie had a feeling that he wasn't about to go down without a fight.

She was right.

"He trusted a mortal with the secrets of our Brotherhood," Arthur hissed.

"Who among us hasn't?" Miss Kiss shot back, "We've all entrusted mortals with our secrets. Centuries have seen different mortals enter this castle. I believe that you once hosted the Queen of England and her sister?"

Several people had to stifle giggles.

"Yes," Arthur growled, "However, none of those mortals were ever so hastily given membership into the Brotherhood. How were they to know that Minerva Banks didn't have an ulterior motive? Who says that she still doesn't?"

"W...what?" Minnie stammered.

Arthur walked towards her raised his hand.

Miss Kiss gasped, Nicolas groaned, Perry cried out, and Victor ran forward.

Minnie found herself speaking against her will.

"I have no ulterior motive to joining the Brotherhood," Minnie monotonically said, "I am not a threat to the Brotherhood."

Her head was spinning.

She was going to vomit.

She doubled over just as the nauseating feeling dispersed.

"What the hell was that?" Minnie eventually croaked.

"A Truth Spell," Arthur declared.

Minnie realized that this was what Victor had used on Felix several months ago – on the day that Minnie had met them. She straightened up and noticed that the air was crackling and popping.

Arthur angrily turned towards Victor.

"Actually, Your Highness," Perry spat, "That would be from me."

"Myself as well," Nicolas agreed, "Minerva is our friend as much as Victor's. That is why all three of us collaborated before agreeing to ask her to join the Brotherhood."

Arthur looked as though he had swallowed a lemon.

"Well, then," Miss Kiss brightly said, "Seeing as

how Nicky and Perry were involved in the decision-making process and seeing as how Minerva Banks poses no threat, I see no reason why she shouldn't be a member of the Brotherhood."

Minnie beamed.

Her smile stretched as she realized that Felix looked furious.

Arthur was quiet for a moment.

"Very well," Arthur eventually boomed, "I will consider it."

"King Arthur," Felix began.

Arthur put his hand up and thundered, "Fortunately, Minerva Banks will be given a chance to prove herself. For this year marks the thirteenth year since our last examination."

Gasps and groans echoed throughout the chamber.

Minnie inwardly shrugged.

She had already taken three tests this week - one more wouldn't hurt.

"The examination will take place here," Arthur continued, "Though it gives me great pain knowing that I will have to once again share my castle with Victor, Nicolas, and Perenelle. I will therefore see to it that the examination takes no longer than a week to complete."

Minnie heard sighs of relief and was astonished.

The test was going to take a week to complete?

Why was that a relief?

"As much as I would love to throw them into the dungeons," Arthur went on, "I will permit Nicolas, Perenelle, Victor, and Minerva to stay in the guest chambers."

Victor looked delighted.

"The traditional rules apply," Arthur declared, "The one who receives the lowest score will be removed from the Brotherhood. All others will remain."

He peered down at Minnie and coldly said, "Minerva Banks, your fate in the Brotherhood of Merlin rests in your ability; or lack thereof."

Felix snickered.

Arthur stretched his hand out and added, "I'm going to need your pin."

Minnie glanced down at the golden 'M' pin that she had worn every day for the past three months. There was no way that she was letting Arthur confiscate it.

As such, she lifted her head and said, "No."

"What did you just say?"

"No," Minnie repeated.

His temple was throbbing. He reached out and snatched the pin, ripping a part of her shirt in the process. Minnie cried out and immediately tapped her scabbard. She withdrew her sword just as Victor withdrew his own. He had leapt in front of her in one fluid motion.

"Touch her again," Victor snarled, "And my blade touches your throat."

Arthur completely ignored him.

"Minerva Banks," Arthur growled, "If you really want to join the Brotherhood of Merlin then I suggest that you learn our creed. We fight together. We fall together."

A ball of red light crashed into Victor's chest.

He was thrown back into Minnie's wheelchair.

The force sent the chair flying. Minnie screamed as she fell to the ground. She wasn't able to catch herself. The side of her head hit the stone floor and the world faded away.

CHAPTER THREE

"Minerva?"

Minnie's world was a sickening, spiraling, blur.

"Minerva?"

Victor whispered her name once more.

She blinked and saw that he was crouching next to her.

"I'm fine," Minnie croaked.

He helped her back into her wheelchair.

Perry examined her before ensuring that she was alright.

At least, she was physically alright.

"Okay," Minnie blurted out, "I have some questions."

"Go on."

"What was that all about?" Minnie asked, "Where exactly are we? Who were the other cloaked people standing on the dais? What is the examination? Am I going to have to take it? Is it really going to take a week? Why are people so relieved about the fact that it's going to take a week? Does that mean that we're stuck here for a week? What the hell is Arthur's problem?"

Nicolas provided the answers, "We're at Castle Tintagel– located in Cornwall, England. It is the home of the Brotherhood of Merlin. What you just witnessed was a fairly standard meeting of the Brotherhood. The other cloaked people were the Knights. The examination consists of individual challenges that are made to test our ability. You're going to have to take it if you wish to be a member of the Brotherhood. It really *is* going to last a week. People are relieved because there have been challenges that have surpassed months. We *are* going to be stuck here for the week. Arthur's problem is Victor."

"And you," Victor pointed out.

"And me," Nicolas agreed.

Minnie's heart was thundering.

She buried her face in her hands as she tried to pull herself together.

An hour ago, she had been working on her essay.

Now, she was in a castle halfway across the world, she was going to be stuck there for a week, and she had to go through a rigorous examination to become an official member of the Brotherhood of Merlin. It was too much to take in.

To make things worse, she still had dozens of other questions.

She only looked up when she realized that Victor had wandered away. He began to walk around the room, seemingly in a daze.

Minnie was about to call his name when Perry

whispered, "Leave him. It's been years since we've been back here."

"Wait," Minnie slowly said, "I understand why Victor doesn't live here but-"

"Why don't Nicolas and I live here?" Perry sadly finished.

Minnie nodded.

"It's a long story," Nicolas admitted, "I'm curious to see why Arthur ended up summoning us here. He has gone out of his way for decades to summon us somewhere else."

"He had neither the time nor the patience," Miss Kiss explained, "We had just sat down to dinner when Felix let it slip about Minnie."

"Let it slip?" Minnie repeated, "Oh, yeah...I'm sure that it was an accident."

Miss Kiss sympathetically smiled and said, "Arthur was so angry that he immediately ordered us into the chamber and summoned the four of you."

Minnie was barely listening.

Her head was still spinning from everything that had happened.

Perry seemed to notice for she called Victor's name.

Victor turned.

"Perhaps we ought to retreat to the guest chambers?" Perry pointedly asked.

Victor looked disappointed but ultimately

nodded.

Minnie hardly paid attention as she followed the group through the castle. Her mind was too busy buzzing with dread and anticipation. At one point, the four stopped to use a rather modern bathroom. They also used a modern elevator. Minnie was stunned that the modern facilities didn't seem to clash with the medieval décor. It blended right into the beauty of the castle. Minnie screeched to a halt as she realized that the others had stopped.

They were staring at a large tapestry on the wall.

Minnie slowly wheeled over and stared at it.

The tapestry depicted a powerful man. Minnie was shocked at how well his skin matched hers; right down to the hue. Waves of silver hair merged with a long, silver, beard. His eyes seemed to hold every color in the world. A golden 'M' was pinned to his magnificent set of robes. Minnie could only stare at the tapestry in wonder.

At long last, she whispered, "Who is that?"

"What do you mean, 'Who is that?'"

Minnie glanced over her shoulder.

Arthur and the Knights were standing behind her.

He spoke as if it was obvious:

"That's *Merlin*."

He was staring at Minnie as if she was a toddler.

"Dear God," Arthur cried, "Hasn't Victor taught

you anything?"

Nicolas made a small noise.

Arthur scoffed and walked away. The Knights hurried after him. Minnie turned her attention back to the tapestry. She was stunned.

"Merlin's black?" Minnie finally whispered.

Victor gave a start and nodded.

"Merlin," Minnie croaked, "*The* Merlin is black?"

"He *was*."

Victor was giving her a weird look.

Minnie's heart was racing.

"Why didn't you tell me?" Minnie exclaimed.

Her eyes were stinging.

She started to tremble.

Victor shrugged and said, "I didn't think that it was relevant."

"You didn't think that it was relevant?" Minnie repeated, "You didn't think that it was relevant to tell me that the greatest sorcerer in the world had the same skin color as me?"

Her voice cracked.

This was amazing!

She forgot about her pain and nausea. She continued to excitedly shake as she gaped at the tapestry. The greatest sorcerer in the world had the same skin color as her!

Minnie was trying to contain herself.

Minnie was *failing* to contain herself.

She let out a small laugh.

Nicolas, Perry, and Victor smiled.

Minnie flushed as she realized that she was geeking out.

That still didn't stop her from pulling out her phone. She took a picture of herself next to the tapestry. Minnie couldn't exactly share it with anyone else but she was still going to keep it.

The group continued on.

They finally reached the guest chambers.

Nicolas and Perry took one room.

Victor and Minnie took the other.

It was as if somebody had taken her old college dormitory, had replaced the walls with stone, and had added medieval décor. The only differences were a pair of glass double doors that led to a balcony and a third door that led to an attached bathroom.

That alone pulled Minnie out of her daze.

"What am I going to do?" Minnie cried, "I don't have enough medical supplies for a week!"

"Relax," Victor gently said, "I do."

Minnie gave a start and asked, "You have enough of my medical supplies for a week?"

Victor rubbed the back of his neck and mumbled, "I have enough for three months."

Minnie's jaw dropped.

She only closed her mouth when she realized that it wasn't the weirdest thing that she had heard in the past hour. Victor sheepishly pulled something from his pocket. Minnie squinted and realized that it was a miniscule backpack.

"Great," Minnie teased, "Let me just grab my microscope!"

Victor grinned and said, "I'm an inventor, remember?"

He went into the bathroom and came back with a handful of water. He dumped it onto the miniscule backpack and it immediately enlarged to the size of a massive suitcase.

"This is my emergency kit," Victor cheerfully said, "I have ten outfits for each of us, three months of your medical supplies, an emergency phone, an emergency laptop, three emergency credit cards, and an emergency wad of cash. The bowls in the kitchen will automatically refill with food and water so Rasputin will be fine."

Minnie dazedly nodded.

Victor declared that he was going to go check something. Minnie nodded and he slipped into the corridor without another word.

It took Minnie a while to fully accept her fate. Nicolas and Perry dropped by to ensure that she was alright. Perry comforted Minnie until she finally came to terms with the fact that she was going to be stuck in the castle for a week. Perry sympathetically patted her arm before leaving her to her thoughts.

Victor returned a few minutes later to find Minnie feverishly typing on the laptop.

"I can't wait to show you everything," Victor excitedly said, "The ballroom, the library, the kitchen, the courtyards, the armories..."

Minnie nodded to acknowledge that she was listening.

"Come on," Victor bracingly said, "Aren't you excited?"

"Ummm...no," Minnie admitted, "No, no. Excited isn't the feeling that most people would have if they were forced into a week-long competition against their will."

Yet she had a small smile on her face.

"Arthur could force us to clean the lavatories against our will," Victor declared, "I would still be excited."

He flopped onto his bed and whispered, "I really missed this place."

"I can tell," Minnie amusedly said.

Victor propped himself up on his elbow and said, "So, stop typing on thine modern-age technology and let's go explore."

"I can't," Minnie retorted, "I need to email my professors."

"Why?"

"I need to let them know that I'm going to be absent."

Victor stared at her for a moment before saying, "I'm sure that they'll figure it out."

"You don't understand," Minnie sighed, "If I don't give them prior notice, I'll be marked with unexcused absences and my participation grades will plummet! It's only a small percentage of my overall grades but it's enough to count! Not to mention that I won't be able to hand in any of my work *or* redo the tests."

Her voice had escalated with each word.

Minnie ultimately buried her face in her hands.

She only looked up when she realized that Victor hadn't said anything.

In fact, Victor was looking at her as though she had sprung a second head.

"What?" Minnie snapped.

"Minerva," Victor slowly said, "You could die in the next few days."

"Victor, no!"

The door to the room had burst open. Perry marched inside. She pushed Victor right off of the bed and sat on the edge. Victor crashed to the ground and looked momentarily dazed.

At long last, he muttered, "Come on in."

"Don't mind if I do," Perry snapped, "Has anyone ever told you that you're horrible at reassuring people?"

Minnie raised her hand.

Victor pulled himself to his knees and grunted, "I'm just trying to advise Minerva to have her priorities in line. Failing college is nothing compared to the prospect of dying."

Minnie's heart was racing.

"That's it," Perry snapped, "Get out."

"Excuse me?"

"Get out."

"Of my own room?"

"Yep," Perry bit, "I'm commandeering it."

Victor opened his mouth but realized that it was better to not argue. Perry shoved him out into the corridor and closed the door.

Minnie managed a weak smile.

Perry put her hand behind her head.

"'Ooh, I'm Victor,'" Perry mockingly said, "'Look at me; I have a ponytail. Don't worry about your hard-earned grades, Minerva. You'll most likely die in the next few days anyway.'"

Minnie doubled over laughing.

"I DON'T SOUND LIKE THAT!"

Victor's irate voice came through the door.

"YEAH," Perry called back, "YOU DO!"

The women giggled as they heard huffs and grunts from the other side.

Minnie eventually used the bathroom and changed into a comfy set of pajamas. She flopped into her bed and stared up at the ceiling.

"So," Minnie finally said, "Why does Arthur hate Victor?"

"Victor's an Antagonist."

"But he hasn't done anything bad," Minnie cried.

"He led to Merlin's death," Perry pointed out, "That's enough for Arthur."

"So he's held a sixteen-hundred-year-old grudge?"

"Mmhm."

Minnie shook her head.

"Are you scared?"

Perry's whisper floated across the room.

"No," Minnie lied.

"Minnie, I'm a mind-reader."

Minnie sighed before grumbling, "Then why even ask?"

"I wanted to see what you would say."

"I'm terrified," Minnie confessed, "Alright? I'm completely and utterly terrified!"

"I understand why," Perry gently said, "Just know that you can do this."

Minnie took a deep breath and nodded.

She could do this.

CHAPTER FOUR

A large crash jolted Minnie from her nightmares.

She was in her wheelchair in an instant. She wheeled over and opened the door, only to be pulled back by Perry. Two figures raced past her. Victor ducked and narrowly avoided a bright blue ball of light. He turned and sent two balls of purple light towards his attacker. Nicolas was able to dodge them. Minnie's jaw dropped as she realized that the two brothers were fighting. She reached for her scabbard but Perry smiled and stopped her.

It dawned on Minnie that Nicolas and Victor were smiling as well. Nevertheless, they continued to throw bursts of energy at one another. They soared through the air, bounced off of the walls, hopped onto windowsills, and knocked over suits of armor. The two had drawn a crowd of spectators. Minnie saw that they were smiling as well. A few even laughed.

"It's been too long," Miss Kiss whispered.

Perry nodded in agreement. The crowd followed the two brothers to the balcony that overlooked the entrance hall. Victor hopped onto the railing and swallowed as Nicolas advanced towards him. A smirk spread across Victor's face as he leapt right off of the railing. His hands caught the bottom of the chandelier. He swung for a moment before ultimately slipping and falling into the entrance hall.

Minnie shouted Victor's name.

She peered over the railing and saw that Victor was lying on his back. He looked dazed and battered but otherwise unharmed. In fact, he was cracking up. Nicolas and Perry helped Minnie down the stone staircase. The rest of the crowd flooded after them.

Victor was still lying on the ground.

He let out a loud cheer before crying, "It's great to be home!"

Several people laughed and whooped.

"This isn't your home anymore."

Everyone immediately hushed.

Arthur had entered the hall with a woman at his side.

"Thanks, King Buzzkill," Victor muttered.

"No need to thank me," Arthur remarked, "After all, you were the one who—"

"Alright," Nicolas sharply said, "That's enough."

Arthur merely smirked.

Minnie focused her attention on the woman standing next to him. She would have been quite beautiful, had it not been for the scowl that permanently resided on her face.

"Hey, Gwen," Perry spoke up, "How are y—?"

"You will refer to me by my proper title."

Perry gave a start at the woman's interjection. Fortunately, Victor seemed to know exactly what to do. He leapt to his feet before dipping into a low bow.

"Good morrow," Victor eloquently said, "Your Most Beautiful And Generous Majesty, Queen Gwenevere. Tell me, how goeth Sir Lancelot?"

Perry struggled to repress a laugh.

Nicolas looked both amused and exasperated.

Miss Kiss simply looked amused.

Minnie carefully watched as a trace of fear crossed Gwen's face. It quickly dissolved into a combination of anger and embarrassment. Victor straightened up and innocently smiled.

"Come along, dear," Gwen muttered.

She and Arthur marched away. Snickers echoed throughout the entrance hall.

"Should I even ask?" Minnie questioned.

"Gwenevere is Arthur's wife," Miss Kiss explained, "Though she's more acquainted with his Knights than she is with him – particularly Lance."

Minnie got the gist.

Everyone retreated back to their rooms to use the bathroom, take a shower, and get dressed. Minnie then followed Victor down to a large dining hall. Once again, Minnie was reminded of New Quartz University. There were even buffet counters where people were helping themselves. The only difference was that unlike the barely passable grub at her college, this food actually looked delicious. Victor helped carry her plate over to a table in the dining area. Nicolas, Perry, and Miss Kiss joined them.

"So, Victor," Perry slyly said, "How did you sleep?"

"Fantastically," Victor remarked, "Thank you for asking."

Nicolas chuckled and said, "I finally let him into our room around midnight."

The four continued to make small talk as they ate their divine breakfast. Minnie couldn't help but to notice that many people were glaring at their table. The others noticed as well.

Felix eventually walked over.

He held his head high as he loudly said, "Do be careful, Kissinger! You don't want their slime to get onto your food!"

Several people laughed. They laughed even harder when a bowl of porridge hit the back of Felix's head. He spun around to fight the person who had thrown it.

In the end, Felix ended up towering over a seven-year-old boy. Minnie's first impression was that the child clearly needed to be better attended to; not because of his behavior but because of his appearance. Minnie wasn't sure if his hair was dirty blonde or if it was simply filthy. She decided that it was both. It was covered in mud and grease, as were his clothes. His silver eyes were sparkling.

The boy cheekily spoke up, "Sorry, Felix; I

mistook you for a pile of trash!"

The walls of the dining hall shook as everyone roared with laughter.

Felix stepped forward but Victor stepped in front of the boy. He had leapt up from the table so fast that his chair had been thrown backwards.

"Keep moving," Victor warned.

Felix sneered but ultimately shuffled away.

Victor turned to the boy and raised an eyebrow.

The boy merely shrugged and said, "That 'slime' comment was uncalled for."

"Speaking of slime," Victor amusedly said, "What have you gotten yourself into?"

The boy grinned and said, "I was playing outside. You *do* remember what 'playing' is, don't you?"

"I remember that I was always clean," Victor retorted.

"Your memory needs a bit of work," Nicolas laughed, "You were so filthy that I once forbade you from entering the castle until the stench wore off."

Everyone laughed.

The boy stepped forward before awkwardly pausing.

Victor raised an eyebrow and asked, "You're not going to try to hug me, are you?"

"Of course not!"

"Good."

There was a moment's pause.

The boy ultimately raced forward and wrapped his arms around Victor's stomach.

Victor chuckled and returned the hug.

"It's good to see you, kid," Victor gently said, "I missed you."

"I missed you, too."

The boy pulled back before glancing at Minnie.

"This is my friend, Minerva Banks," Victor explained, "Minerva, this is Dmitri."

"Nice to meet you," Dmitri politely said.

He held out his hand and Minnie reluctantly shook it. She quickly wiped her hand on her napkin. Perry soaked her own napkin in water and began fussing over Dmitri, much to the child's dismay. Victor smirked as he picked his chair back up and sat down once more. Dmitri finally wriggled away from Perry and sat on Victor's other side.

Victor rubbed his back and grumbled, "Don't ever make me dive in front of you again."

"Sorry," Dmitri cried, "Who knew that Felix would be mad when struck with porridge?"

"You learn new things about him every day," Miss Kiss teased.

Nicolas pulled a vial from his pocket and handed it to Victor. He swallowed the contents in a single gulp and sighed with relief.

"Get used to that taste, Victor!"

The group looked up and saw that Arthur was

standing nearby.

"You're going to need all of the pain relievers that you can get," Arthur boomed, "My fellow members of the Brotherhood of Merlin...and Minerva...please follow me to the entrance of the first dungeon! The first challenge is about to begin!"

There was a large amount of commotion and confusion as everyone flooded after him.

Minnie had to wait twice before there was finally enough room in the elevator.

Victor squeezed in next to her. When the elevator finally reached the lowest level, the members of the Brotherhood popped out like clowns from a miniature car. Minnie found a bathroom and quickly used it. She then followed Victor down the dark corridor until they reached an ordinarily looking door. A glass window allowed the Brotherhood to look into an empty chamber.

Arthur gained the crowd's attention before rumbling, "The first challenge shall test your endurance and stamina! One by one, you will all enter this chamber. With each passing minute, you will feel increasing waves of pain. Should the pain become unbearable, you will simply need to leave the room. A single point will be rewarded for each minute that you survive."

Felix stepped forward and whispered something.

Arthur smirked and said, "Seeing as how

Minerva Banks is our distinguished guest, I say that she should have the honor of going first."

"Oh, thanks," Minnie dryly said, "I feel so honored."

"Step forward!"

Minnie stared at him.

"Wheel forward!"

Minnie reluctantly complied. She entered the room and heard Arthur slam the door behind her. She didn't feel anything for a few moments. After a quarter of an hour, however, she was starting to uncomfortably squirm. White hot pain was searing through her entire body. It was as if pins and needles were piercing each and every part of her skin. Nevertheless, she remained strong. She glanced through the window and saw her friends cheering her on. Minnie's heart lifted and she pushed the pain away. Another twenty minutes passed, each more daunting than the last. She doubled over and gritted her teeth. She thought of her worst days at the hospital.

In the end, she lasted forty-seven minutes before desperately wheeling out into the corridor. Nicolas handed her a large vial. She gratefully accepted it and felt a sense of relief as the liquid trickled down her throat. The pain ceased within seconds.

"Are you okay?" Victor worriedly asked.

Minnie nodded.

She had no idea whether she had done well or had utterly failed.

It turned out to be the former.

Other members of the Brotherhood reluctantly took their turns. Yet they didn't last nearly as long as Minnie. Nicolas, Perry, and Miss Kiss each staggered out within the first thirty-five minutes. Even Arthur ended up quickly surrendering. For a moment, it seemed as though Minnie had everyone beat.

And then Victor stepped into the chamber.

Minnie and the others peered through the window and watched as he calmly sat down in the middle of the floor. Several minutes passed. Those minutes turned into an entire hour without so much as a single movement from Victor. He was just sitting there.

Arthur and the Knights exchanged glances. The rest of the Brotherhood was murmuring to one another. Oddly enough, Nicolas, Perry, and Miss Kiss seemed unperturbed.

Upon seeing Arthur's scowl, the Knights began to offer suggestions:

"Perhaps the room is broken?"

"He could be cheating?"

"He's an inventor."

"That's true."

"Indeed."

"Did he invent something to stop the pain?"

Yet a thorough magical inspection showed that the room was working and that Victor was experiencing the pain; he simply wasn't reacting.

Arthur didn't respect this answer.

He angrily wrenched the door open.

"Get out," Arthur growled.

"Nah," Victor easily said, "I can probably last another hour or two."

"GET OUT!"

Victor shrugged and said, "I'm not leaving unless I'm dragged out."

Arthur charged into the room and immediately regretted it. He fell to his knees and let out a chilling scream. He was finally able to crawl back into the corridor. His entire body trembled and he looked as though he was going to be sick. The Knights all crowded around him.

"I'm fine," Arthur hissed, "I'm fine!"

Felix was the one who ultimately helped him to his feet.

Arthur's face was as red as his cloak. Sweat was rolling down his neck. His crown was askew and bits of spittle were on the corner of his lip.

The rest of the Brotherhood awkwardly looked at anywhere other than their king.

Minnie was stunned.

Arthur had only been in the room for a few

seconds.

Victor had already been in the room for an hour and was going on strong.

Arthur spun around and bellowed, "GET OUT!"

Everyone jumped and gasped.

"No," Victor simply said.

Arthur turned to face Nicolas.

He seemed to get the message for he stepped towards the doorway.

"Are you alright?" Nicolas called.

Victor nodded.

"The minute that you're not," Nicolas firmly said, "You need to leave."

Victor nodded once more.

Forty minutes passed until the tension was unbearable. Minnie and Perry clung onto one another as they stared through the window. Victor looked slightly uncomfortable but otherwise cheerful. He was even humming.

One of the Knights shook his head and muttered, "He should be dead."

"That's the understatement of the millennium," Arthur angrily said.

Another thirty minutes passed.

"Hey, R," Victor called, "I don't suppose that I can take a bathroom break?"

"NO!"

Minnie was fairly certain that Arthur was going

to have a stroke.

"It must be that spot," Arthur concluded, "He's been sitting there for an hour and a half! I guarantee that it's that spot. How else can he survive?"

Victor coolly raised an eyebrow.

He leapt to his feet and did a small twirl.

He remained stone-faced as he began to dance around the room.

Minnie, Dmitri, and Perry cracked up.

"WHAT THE HELL ARE YOU DOING?" Arthur shrieked.

"I'm dancing," Victor replied, "In order to prove that it's not the spot."

"HOW ARE YOU DOING THIS?"

"Dancing?" Victor innocently asked, "Oh, it's rather simple..."

"HOW ARE YOU NOT IN PAIN?"

"I *am* in pain," Victor shot back, "I'm in *excruciating* pain."

"THEN HOW ARE YOU ABLE TO ENDURE IT?"

Victor leaned forward and smugly said, "With about sixteen-hundred-years of practice."

He continued to dance until he ended up tripping over his shoelace. He was able to catch himself before he hit the ground. He then shifted so that he was sitting once more.

Meanwhile, Minnie's eyes had widened.

Victor's words were echoing around in her mind.

He had just inadvertently answered a question that Minnie had been wondering for three months. Perry had once stated that she, her husband, and her brother-in-law all had an invisible disability. Perry had openly admitted that she battled depression and that Nicolas was immunocompromised. Victor had changed the subject before his disability had been revealed.

Yet, he had just revealed it.

Minnie glanced at Perry who nodded.

Thirteen more minutes passed.

Victor stood up and calmly exited the room. He dramatically stretched and yawned, earning giggles and chuckles from the rest of the Brotherhood.

"Are you okay?" Minnie asked.

"I'm fine," Victor bracingly said, "Never been better."

Perry still produced a large vial and gave it to him.

Victor greedily drank the contents.

He only paused when he realized that Minnie was staring at him.

"What?" Victor asked.

Minnie jerked her head.

Victor confusedly followed her down the corridor and around the corner. Minnie hesitated as she tried to think of what to say.

"What?" Victor repeated.

"Nothing," Minnie remarked, "It's just..."

"Just what?"

"I thought that twenty-five years of chronic pain was hell," Minnie whispered, "I couldn't imagine sixteen-hundred years of it."

Victor's eyes widened.

His face ultimately broke out into an impressed smile.

"How did you figure it out?" Victor wondered.

Minnie recounted what he had said in the chamber.

"Yeah," Victor sheepishly said, "I suppose that that was a bit obvious, wasn't it?"

He glanced around before whispering, "Would you mind keeping it a secret? Nicolas, Perry, Miss Kiss, and Dmitri are the only other ones who know."

"O...of course," Minnie stammered, "But why?"

Victor shrugged and said, "I don't want anyone to judge."

"Is that why you never told me?"

Victor didn't deny it.

"Oh, yeah," Minnie sarcastically said, "Because I would *completely* judge someone because of their disability. That's exactly the type of person that I am!"

"Alright, alright," Victor chuckled, "Point taken."

The two glanced up as Perry practically flew around the corner.

"Dmitri passed out," Perry cried, "Hurry!"

Victor and Minnie raced after her. They pushed through the crowd and peered through the large window. Sure enough, Dmitri was lying in the middle of the chamber.

Victor quickly entered and picked the poor boy up.

He carried Dmitri out into the corridor.

Nicolas combined two vials of liquid and poured them down the child's throat.

Dmitri stirred with a groan.

"Are you okay?" Victor gently asked.

"Fine," Dmitri grunted, "I really hate Arthur."

"I'm standing right here," Arthur coolly said.

Dmitri didn't so much as flinch.

Instead, he stood up and simply said, "I hate you."

Arthur let out a bark of laughter.

"Like I really care what some seven-year-old has to say," Arthur snarled.

His Knights chortled.

"Go on," Dmitri snapped, "Laugh. It doesn't change the fact that you're deliberately torturing the Brotherhood of Merlin. I'm sure the old guy would have loved that. I mean, it's not as though his philosophies were based on peace and pacifism."

Whispers and murmurs rang throughout the chamber.

"I wonder what he would think," Dmitri

continued, "If he was here today?"

"That's a good question," Arthur admitted, "Unfortunately, thanks to Victor, we will never know. Who's up next?"

And so, the next member of the Brotherhood reluctantly entered the chamber.

The next few hours were heinously uncomfortable. On three different occasions, Victor had to enter the room to drag people out. The entire corridor was filled with the vile stench of sweat and vomit. Onlookers were only permitted to leave to use the bathroom.

In the end, Victor was rewarded with 145 points.

Arthur rewarded himself with 100 points, though everyone knew that he hadn't even lasted half an hour in the chamber.

Minnie didn't fare too badly with 47 points.

Nicolas, Perry, and Miss Kiss respectively received 29, 35, and 31 points.

Most of the Brotherhood ranged from 20 to 40 points.

Unfortunately, Dmitri only received 3 points.

He furiously blinked back tears.

"Hey, hey," Minnie gently said, "It's alright."

Dmitri sniffed and nodded.

"At least you did well," Dmitri weakly said.

"Yes," Arthur boomed, "You did quite well, Minerva Banks!"

"Thanks."

Arthur nodded before saying, "Our next challenge is about to begin!"

Few people were able to suppress groans. Everyone was already physically, mentally, and emotionally exhausted. Arthur ignored the groans and walked over to the second door.

"This challenge is designed to test your physical ability," Arthur declared.

"Why do I have the feeling that I'm not going to like this?" Minnie muttered.

Sure enough, Arthur eloquently said, "You shall each run through a rigorous obstacle course. Completing the obstacle course in under an hour will earn you one-hundred points. Two hours shall earn you fifty points. Three hours shall earn you twenty-five points and so on. Does anyone have any questions?"

Minnie raised her hand and skeptically said, "I don't suppose that this obstacle course is wheelchair accessible?"

Arthur didn't need to answer.

"Of course not," Minnie sighed.

Arthur mimicked an apologetic voice, "I'm so sorry, Minerva, but I'm afraid that since you cannot complete this challenge, you cannot earn any points."

Minnie rolled her eyes.

Victor, Nicolas, Perry, Miss Kiss, and Dmitri all

grumbled and groaned. Yet there was nothing that they could do about it.

"Fine," Minnie eventually said, "It gives me more time to work on my essay."

She patted Victor on the arm and added, "Have fun."

Minnie wheeled back up to their room. She flopped onto the bed but didn't so much as look at the laptop. She was too tired to even think straight...

She jerked awake as the door to the room burst open.

"Sorry," Victor apologized.

Minnie swore and cried, "Are you alright?"

He was battered, bruised, and bloody. His one eye was almost completely swollen shut. A large gash was on his neck. His wrist was twice the normal size.

"I'm fine," Victor dismissively said, "The next challenge is about to begin."

Minnie groaned and climbed back into her wheelchair. She quickly used the bathroom before reluctantly following him. She fretted over an exasperated Victor's injuries on their way back down to the dungeons. She realized that the other members of the Brotherhood didn't look any better. Dmitri's hair was caked with blood, Perry was limping, Nicolas was missing several teeth, and Miss Kiss was clutching two broken ribs.

They grouped around the third door.

"I bet you're all wondering what's in here," Arthur mysteriously said.

Perry took one look at him and muttered, "I'm not."

Arthur glared at her.

"What is it?" Victor whispered.

Perry opened her mouth but Arthur interrupted, "Does everyone have a weapon?"

Minnie instinctively ensured that her scabbard was still in tact. It was, even if she couldn't see it. She watched as the other members of the Brotherhood grabbed their own weapons.

Dmitri hesitated before admittedly saying, "I don't have a weapon."

"Victor," Arthur barked, "Give Dmitri your sword."

"Yeah, that's safe," Victor muttered.

Nevertheless, he handed the sword to the child.

"Dmitri," Arthur boomed, "You're first."

"Hang on," Victor exclaimed, "Aren't you going to tell us what he's facing?"

"You'll find out in time."

Dmitri hesitated before opening the door and entering a dark tunnel. Arthur immediately shut the door behind him.

There was nothing left to do but wait.

Minnie genuinely hated waiting.

The seconds crawled by.

She anxiously drummed her fingers against the arm of her chair, only stopping when Victor's fingers intertwined with hers.

"It's alright," Victor whispered, "He's going to be alright."

Minnie wasn't sure which one of them he was reassuring.

She squeezed his hand and he squeezed back.

The golden light appeared and Minnie allowed herself to be distracted by it.

It was better than thinking about Dmitri.

She saw a very irate Arthur out of the corner of her eye.

Dmitri burst through the door ten minutes later. He was flushed and breathless but otherwise unharmed. Victor reached towards him and demanded to know what had happened.

Dmitri didn't answer and instead cried, "Why would you do that?"

He was facing Arthur.

Arthur merely smirked and set the next person in. They came out looking just as shocked as Dmitri was. As did the third. The fourth was visibly shaken. The fifth was in tears.

Nicolas and Victor respectively went in and came out looking horrified.

Perry emerged looking furious.

"Oh, yeah," Perry snapped, "Because Merlin

would have wanted that."

"Wanted what?" Minnie pressed, "What's in there?"

Arthur's voice drowned out Perry's answer.

"Tut tut," Arthur teased, "Nobody has earned any points so far."

He glanced over his shoulder before crying, "Felix!"

Felix immediately snapped to attention. He pulled out his sword and confidently entered the tunnel. The dysfunctional group apprehensively waited.

Felix emerged ten minutes later.

Several people screamed. Perry let out a deep sigh. Minnie felt faint. Dmitri buried his face into Victor's side. He tightly hugged the boy while staring at Felix in horror. Nicolas mirrored his expression.

Felix was holding the decapitated head of a unicorn.

CHAPTER FIVE

The dark corridor was spinning.

Minnie groaned and doubled over.

The other members of the Brotherhood weren't faring any better. Several became sick and a few crumpled to the ground. Victor reached over and put his hand on Minnie's shoulder. The golden light twisted around them. She took a shuddering breath before straightening up.

"You okay?" Victor whispered.

Minnie shook her head.

Her eyes fell upon the unicorn's head that Felix had so carelessly tossed to the ground.

Victor gently grabbed her chin and forced her to look away.

"So," Minnie croaked, "Unicorns are real?"

Victor nodded.

"Shouldn't they usually be attached to a body?" Minnie weakly asked.

"That's the challenge," Victor bitterly said, "In order to gain points, you need to bring forth the head of one of the most innocent creatures in the world."

"Makes sense," Minnie rasped.

Dmitri pulled away from Perry and cried, "Right?"

The seven-year-old glared at Arthur as he

sarcastically said, "I bet that that's exactly what Merlin would have wanted."

Dmitri then turned to Nicolas and cheerfully said, "Oh, hullo there, Merlin! What are you doing today?"

Nicolas played along.

"Why, I'm just slaughtering unicorns," Nicolas rumbled, "Say, would you mind stepping into this pain chamber?"

"One moment, Merlin," Dmitri quipped, "First, I need to hurt the man who was like your very own son."

He began to lightly hit Victor.

Several people let out weak laughs.

Arthur rolled his eyes and stepped forward.

"Say, Merlin," Arthur snarled, "Can you share some of your valuable philosophies of the world? No? Oh, that's right! The man who was like your very own son ultimately ended up leading to your death."

Nicolas pretended to stroke a long beard as he said, "Arthur, have I ever mentioned that you were my least favorite son?"

The resulting laughs immediately dissipated as Arthur glared at everyone.

"Minerva," Arthur spat, "You're next!"

Minnie glanced at Victor who merely offered a shrug.

She took a deep breath and entered the dark

corridor. She jumped as the door slammed behind her. She apprehensively wheeled forward. Torches lit the way as she went deeper and deeper into the wall. She eventually came out into a large grove.

Her jaw practically touched the floor.

She was facing at least two dozen unicorns.

There are three types of girls in elementary school: the girls who are obsessed with dogs, the girls who are obsessed with horses, and the girls who are obsessed with horses that have horns jutting out of their foreheads. Minerva Banks had been in the last category.

As such, she was having a hard time containing herself.

Her heart was racing as she looked around in wonder. It immediately sank as she realized that the unicorns were mourning. She flinched as she spotted the lifeless, headless, body lying in the grass.

One of the unicorns noticed her and whispered, "Another one approaches!"

Its voice was silky smooth.

The unicorns became very still. They were all apprehensively staring at her, as if waiting to defend themselves. Of course! They thought that she was going to behead one of them, just as Felix had done. Minnie had absolutely no intention of doing so.

She slowly tapped her scabbard, causing it to become visible. The unicorns reared back but ultimately relaxed as Minnie threw the scabbard to the ground.

"I...I don't want to hurt you," Minnie croaked. "I'm sorry that Felix..."

She broke off.

The unicorns seemed to understand.

Minnie sadly stared down at the body and asked, "Is there anything that I can do?"

She knew that it was a stupid question and regretted asking it.

Her eyes widened as she realized that small dots of golden light were circling the fallen body. A sudden flash caused Minnie to turn her face away. When she looked back, she realized that the body was gone.

"W...where did it go?" Minnie squeaked.

One of the unicorns offered a simple explanation:

"On."

Minnie's voice was an octave higher than usual as she said, "Okay."

The unicorn lifted its head and cried, "We have mourned the loss of our fallen and will continue to cherish their spirit for ages to come. Yet, we must move forward, lest our souls be corrupted by sadness."

The atmosphere of the room changed dramatically. Though the unicorns still seemed wary of Minnie, they also seemed perfectly content with their lives.

One of the unicorns stepped forward and gently asked, "Are you from the Brotherhood of Merlin?"

Minnie opened her mouth but could not speak.

The unicorn repeated its question.

"I...I...w...want to be," Minnie stammered.

The unicorn surveyed her before saying, "In order to earn points for this challenge, you must take a unicorn's head back to the Brotherhood."

Minnie shivered.

"Don't worry," Minnie eventually croaked, "I'm not going to hurt any of you."

"You won't earn any points."

Minnie sighed but accepted this. She picked up her scabbard, turned around, and started to wheel back into the tunnel. She then stopped and turned back to the beautiful grove.

"Okay," Minnie gushed, "This is going to be the geekiest thing that I've said in a while, including that one time that I wheeled up to a group of superheroes and asked to join. I was just wondering if...if I could...pet you?"

The last two words came out in a squeak.

The unicorn looked apprehensive.

"Yeah," Minnie awkwardly said, "That was weird."

She apologized and started to wheel away once more.

"We will permit it."

Minnie spun around so fast that her wheelchair nearly tipped. The unicorn dipped its head and allowed Minnie to stroke its long mane. She learned that its name was Rainwater and that it was over seven-thousand-years-old. She wasn't aware of how much time it passed until a figure emerged from the tunnel. Minnie and the unicorns tensed.

"What are you *doing*?" Victor amusedly asked.

Minnie's face burned as she quickly removed her hand from Rainwater's head.

"Nothing," Minnie squeaked, "I was just..."

She awkwardly broke off before asking, "What are *you* doing?"

He stuffed his hands into his pockets and said, "Arthur wanted me to make sure that you didn't get trampled on. I didn't mean to interrupt."

"Sorry," Minnie bashfully said.

"You have no business to judge her, Victor Flamel." Rainwater declared, "I distinctly recall you riding on our backs when you were younger."

It was Victor's turn to flush.

Minnie amusedly raised an eyebrow.

"Alright, alright," Victor mumbled, "Let's go."

Minnie reluctantly gave Rainwater's head one last pat.

She then gasped as something hit her.

"What's wrong?" Victor cried.

"What exactly do I have to do to earn points on this challenge?" Minnie questioned.

Rainwater tensed and whispered, "You must bring the head of a unicorn to the rest of the Brotherhood of Merlin."

"Fine," Minnie cheerfully said, "I'm going to do that!"

Victor cried her name.

"Yes?"

"What are you doing?" Victor exclaimed.

"I'm going to bring the head of a unicorn to the Brotherhood," Minnie explained.

Victor uncertainly stepped forward.

"Minerva," Victor whispered, "You can't kill a unicorn!"

"I'm not," Minnie retorted, "They never said that the head had to be decapitated."

Rainwater let out a small, impressed, grunt.

"Would you mind following me?" Minnie gently asked.

Rainwater dipped its head in agreement.

Victor's face broke out into a grin.

A few moments later, Victor and Minnie entered the dark corridor. Rainwater was behind them. The members of the Brotherhood gasped. Dmitri, Nicolas, Perry, and Miss Kiss smiled.

"There you go," Minnie triumphantly said, "A unicorn's head."

"That doesn't count," Arthur snapped.

"It certainly counts," Rainwater softly said, "For, as you can plainly see, I have a head. In the future, might I suggest making stricter requirements before you involve our species in your sadistic challenges? Merlin would be very disappointed in you."

Arthur looked as though he had been punched.

Rainwater bid farewell to Minnie before trotting back into the tunnel.

Minnie triumphantly glanced around. She realized that Felix had hidden behind one of the Knights. She also realized that the other unicorn's dismembered head had disappeared.

Minnie supposed that it had gone 'on' as well.

The remaining members of the Brotherhood stepped into the tunnel and returned with a unicorn of their own. Arthur's temple was throbbing as he begrudgingly awarded them points.

"That's all for today," Arthur finally spat, "We will meet here tomorrow at noon. I shall remain in my chamber until then. Dismissed!"

He stomped away without another word, his loyal subjects following him.

A few members of the Brotherhood came up to Minnie and congratulated her. Minnie, Victor, Nicolas, Miss Kiss, and Dmitri followed the group back up to the dining hall. They picked and poked at a roast. The vision of the unicorn's severed head dampened everyone's appetite. Minnie ultimately retreated to her room. She used the bathroom, changed into her pajamas, and climbed into bed. Yet sleep eluded her.

Minnie eventually sat up and climbed back into her wheelchair.

She aimlessly roamed around the corridors of the castle.

She only paused when she heard a beautiful tune.

Somebody was playing a piano.

Minnie followed the sound until she reached a magnificent ballroom. The walls were lined with gold. An enormous chandelier hung from the ceiling. An ebony grand piano sat in the corner. Minnie was shocked when she recognized its player. Victor's eyes were closed as his fingers danced along the keys, seemingly knowing exactly where to go. Minnie slowly wheeled forward. The melody that he was playing was hauntingly beautiful. Minnie didn't recognize it. And yet, she felt as if she had always known it.

Minnie glanced around the room and realized that it must have once contained eloquent balls. Men in their finest suits. Women in dresses with skirts that billowed out. Couples dancing in one another's embrace, gracefully twirling with the music. Children merrily laughing and stepping on one another's feet. Minnie could only imagine how amazing it must have been.

She turned back to Victor and saw that his eyes were still closed.

She went to wheel away but he called her name.

Minnie sheepishly turned back.

Victor's fingers hadn't left the piano, yet his attention was on her.

"I didn't know that you could play," Minnie softly said.

Victor nodded and said, "It's a fine skill to have when you don't want to dance."

Minnie laughed.

She listened to him play for a while longer before saying, "You should honestly join an orchestra. Have you played for anyone else?"

"I've played for Miss Kiss a few times," Victor admitted.

"Miss Kiss?"

Victor nodded and said, "She's a professional singer. She's been doing it for centuries."

He played for a few more minutes before finally finishing.

Minnie applauded before asking, "What song was it?"

"I don't have a title yet," Victor admitted, "I composed it last night."

Minnie gave a start.

"You compose your own music?" Minnie cried, "That's incredible."

Victor proudly smiled.

"When did you start?" Minnie asked.

"When I was young," Victor admitted, "We practically had a different ball each week. I needed an excuse to get out of dancing. I started composing and provided the musical accompaniment. I would sit behind the safety of the piano while the others danced."

A frown crossed his face.

"If it helps," Minnie cried, "I can't dance, either!"

"Oh, I can dance," Victor quickly said.

"Sure, you can."

Victor rose from his seat and said, "I happen to be a fantastic dancer."

"Prove it!"

"Maybe I will."

"You should."

They two glanced up as Perry raced through the doorway.

She paused before saying, "Sorry to interrupt…"

"And yet," Victor lightly said, "You're doing it anyway."

"Theodore's messing with Dmitri," Perry declared.

Victor's face immediately hardened. He sprinted out of the room and the women followed suit. Perry raced in front and led them through the castle corridors.

They took the elevator down to the entrance hall.

What they saw caused Minnie's stomach to twist.

Dmitri was dancing against his own will. It was eerie. His body flopped around as if it was a puppet. Tears were rolling down his face. The Quartet and several other members of the Brotherhood were cackling as they watched him.

"Dmitri," Theodore amusedly said, "Do the can-can."

"Stop," Dmitri pleaded.

Nevertheless, his legs began to individually rise. It was as if invisible strings were pulling them. He eventually lost his balance and crashed to the ground.

"HEY, THEODORE!"

Even Minnie jumped at Victor's outraged roar.

"I have a question for you," Victor snapped.

His fist collided with Theodore's nose. Everyone flinched at the sickening crunch. The villain staggered backwards before ultimately collapsing.

"Did that hurt?" Victor asked.

Theodore clutched his nose and spluttered, "Y...yes!"

Victor honestly couldn't care less. He crouched down and helped Dmitri to his feet. The child was embarrassed but otherwise unharmed.

Minnie let out a small laugh.

She regretted it as eyebrows were immediately raised.

"You're a sixteen-hundred-year-old sorcerer," Minnie cried, "You've mastered one-hundred-and-sixty-nine different spells and you decided to just punch him?"

"It worked," Victor simply said.

"Did my brother really tell you that he's mastered one-hundred-and-sixty-nine different spells?" Felix spoke up, "He's wrong."

Victor rolled his eyes before saying, "I still have the tattoo."

"Because Merlin felt bad," Felix snickered.

He turned to Minnie and said, "He was able to adequately perform one-hundred-and-sixty-eight spells. He was never able to perform the final one."

"Neither did you," Victor shot back, "Mess with Dmitri again and I just might end up mastering it."

He put his arm around the boy's shoulders and led him away.

Minnie and Perry followed.

"You can't do The Push?" Dmitri quipped.

"Not efficiently," Victor admitted, "Probably a good thing, eh?"

Dmitri chuckled before asking, "Can you do it, Perry?"

Perry shook her head.

"What is The Push?" Minnie curiously asked.

"It's a strange sort of spell," Victor explained, "You end up releasing a wall of pure energy all around you. It's been known to bring down entire rooms."

A twisted smile spread across his face.

Perry was mirroring the expression.

Victor's nose abruptly wrinkled and he muttered, "You really need a bath, kid."

Dmitri merely stuck out his tongue.

"Go on," Victor amusedly said.

"No!"

"Yes!"

"No!"

"Yes!"

"Oh, come on," Dmitri complained, "I wanted to get a snack."

"What were you going to get?"

"The chefs made chocolate cake."

"Terrific," Victor cried, "You can eat it after your bath."

"No!"

"Yes!"

"No!"

"Go take a bath!"

"Or what?" Dmitri shot back, "You'll ground me?"

"Don't tempt me!"

Minnie chuckled at the look at Dmitri's face.

"Go take a bath," Minnie advised, "Then you can

have two pieces of cake."

"What?" Victor yelped, "That's not part of the—"

"Deal," Dmitri eagerly said.

He raced away before Victor could protest.

Minnie and Perry giggled at the incredulous look on Victor's face. He eventually shook his head and marched back towards the ballroom. Minnie and Perry followed him.

Victor sat back down at the piano.

He played a different tune – a slow, Russian, waltz.

Minnie proudly smiled.

"Two pieces of cake," Victor muttered.

"Oh, give it a rest," Perry laughed, "You used to eat handfuls of sugar."

"What?" Minnie cackled.

Victor felt that Perry's statement didn't deserve a reply. He intently stared at the piano as he continued to play the beautiful melody. The waltz became more and more intense until the women exchanged concerned glances.

"Victor," Minnie spoke up, "Are you okay?"

"I'm fine."

He continued to harshly play before finally bringing his hands crashing down onto the keys. Minnie and Perry flinched at the terrible noise.

"Do you think that this is the first time?" Victor

quietly asked.

Perry didn't answer.

"The first time for what?" Minnie asked.

"Either way," Perry finally said, "He wouldn't tell you."

"That's what worries me," Victor cried.

He brought his hands down again.

"Easy," Minnie cried.

Victor ignored her.

"You can read his mind," Victor pointed out, "Did you see anything?"

Perry sadly stared at him.

Victor swore and growled, "How bad?"

"Nothing violent," Perry promised, "They just pester him."

Minnie was finally able to piece everything together.

Victor was still angry about Theodore's actions.

He was worried that it had happened before.

"Miss Kiss has been keeping an eye on him," Perry gently said, "So have a few other members."

Victor opened his mouth but closed it.

"I know," Perry sighed, "I know, Victor."

Minnie knew that she was reading his mind.

She wished that she could do the same.

Perry's voice echoed throughout her mind:

'Victor is upset because he cannot be here to constantly protect Dmitri.'

Minnie's heart went out to him. Yet Perry's statement raised a crucial question. Where were Dmitri's parents? She questioningly glanced at Perry.

Perry took a deep breath before sadly saying, "There was a fire."

Minnie winced.

"The funny thing is that we didn't even know that Dmitri existed," Perry explained, "His parents got into a bit of trouble with the Brotherhood."

Victor snorted at the understatement.

"There was a row," Perry went on, "They ultimately left Castle Tintagel and moved to Russia. There was a bit of trouble a few years later. Victor, Nicolas, and I visited Russia. We met them at a quaint little tea shop. We urged them to get out before it was too late."

"Get out of what?" Minnie repeated.

"Don't ask," Perry pleaded.

Minnie hesitated before nodding.

"They refused to listen," Perry continued, "Nicolas, Victor, and I stayed the night a local inn. We woke up and decided to give it another shot. We walked down to their house and saw the blaze. We barged in but it was too late."

Minnie swallowed before croaking, "But weren't they immortal?"

Perry shook her head.

She looked troubled for a moment.

"Anyway," Perry finally said, "They were gone. The house was falling apart all around us. We were about to flee for it when we heard a soft cry for help. We glanced at one another and realized that there was someone else in the house. We heard the cry again. It was a kid. Victor took off running. He bounded right up the flaming staircase. He didn't even notice the burns that he was sustaining. I'm not quite sure what happened after that."

The women glanced at Victor.

He took a deep breath before explaining, "I made it to the top corridor. I called out and the child answered. He was trapped behind a wall of flames. And he said..."

"'Good morning.'"

The three looked up.

A clean Dmitri was standing in the doorway. He was holding several plates of cake. His silver eyes looked wet but he was smiling at Victor.

Victor rose from his seat and gently said, "And I said, 'Good morning.'"

Dmitri nodded and said, "And I said, 'Can you protect me?'"

"And I merely nodded," Victor replied.

"And I said, 'Promise?'"

"And I nodded once more."

"And then I died," Dmitri cheerfully said.

Minnie had chosen a very bad time to take a sip

from her water bottle.

She spat it out and cried, "What?"

"Only for a few minutes," Victor lightly said, "I was able to bring you back."

"*You* didn't bring him back," Perry laughed, "Nicolas happened to have an extra vial of the Elixir of Life. *We* gave it to him ergo *we're* the ones who brought him back."

"*I* was the one who got him to you within the time-limit," Victor teased, "Ergo *I'm* the one who saved his life."

Perry amusedly rolled her eyes.

"Time-limit?" Minnie confusedly asked.

"The Elixir of Life can bring anyone back within thirteen minutes of their death," Perry explained.

Minnie opened her mouth.

Perry answered before the question could be asked, "It also restores all brainwaves and replenishes the other organs. It's as if they had never died."

Minnie nodded.

"It also made me immortal," Dmitri happily said.

Minnie noted that he was taking the topic of his parents' deaths rather well.

Perry's voice wafted through her mind:

'From what he's told us, he didn't exactly have the parents of the year.'

Minnie's heart sank even further. Did this kid ever catch a break?

"Your potion may have made him immortal," Victor jokingly said, "However, I was the one who brought him to you ergo I'm the one who made him immortal."

Dmitri giggled.

"You still owe me," Victor jokingly added.

Dmitri lifted a plate and cried, "I brought you cake."

"Good enough."

Victor snatched the plate and added, "Now, go to bed."

Dmitri sighed.

"We had a long day," Victor pointed out, "Tomorrow's going to be even longer. We're going to need our strength."

"One song?" Dmitri pleaded.

Victor hesitated before nodding.

He sat back down and Dmitri sat next to him.

Minnie glanced out of the corner of her eye and saw that Perry was covering her ears. She raised an eyebrow but didn't comment.

Victor began to gently play.

After a few moments, Minnie realized that she couldn't stop yawning.

She flushed.

Dmitri wasn't doing any better.

It wasn't long before his head hit Victor's arm. Victor smiled and continued to play the slow lullaby.

Minnie stifled a laugh as she realized that he had tricked the boy.

Victor gently shook Dmitri awake and sent him off to bed.

The child didn't argue.

Minnie merely stared at Victor.

"What?"

"Nothing," Minnie cried, "I just never expected you to be the parental-type."

Victor puffed out his chest as he said, "I'm absolutely the parental-type."

Perry tried to hide a laugh behind a cough.

She was unsuccessful.

Victor raised an eyebrow and asked, "Something you'd like to say, Perenelle?"

"You gave Dmitri a sword a few hours ago," Perry exclaimed, "You didn't even hesitate. You just gave a seven-year-old a sword."

"So what?" Victor shot back, "I've given you a sword before. I've given Minerva a sword. I've given random strangers on the streets swords. It's called sharing, Perenelle, and it's a trait that all children should learn. So I kindly shared my sword with Dmitri in the hopes that he would learn about this marvelous trait!"

Minnie shook her head.

"Alright," Victor admittedly said, "I'm not the paternal type. However, I'm still going to protect

Dmitri. A promise is a promise..."

CHAPTER SIX

Dmitri needed all of the protection that he could get.

Minnie sadly peered through the window.

Flames were creeping all around the boy. They licked at his arms and legs. They didn't seem to hurt him, though they did leave different scars.

Dmitri burst into the corridor.

Victor instinctively held out his arms and Dmitri ran into them.

Victor embraced the shaking child and murmured words of comfort.

"Hey, it's okay," Victor whispered, "It's alright."

"N...no...i...it's...not," Dmitri sobbed.

Minnie put a hand on his shoulder and whispered words of comfort. It helped that the other members of the Brotherhood weren't doing as well. They had been down in the dungeons for over an hour. Arthur was eagerly sending them into a chamber that projected one's greatest fears. Minnie sadly recalled what she had thought last night: Dmitri had taken the conversation about his parents' death rather well. Apparently it had just been a farce. The seven-year-old was completely terrified. It took an elixir from Nicolas, a hug from Victor, and a comforting speech from Perry to finally calm him down.

Arthur and the Knights merely laughed.

"Minerva," Arthur called, "You're next!"

Minnie reluctantly wheeled into the chamber.

She blinked and groaned.

She was sitting in a hospital room.

A doctor stepped forward and informed her that the infection had spread. She was going to need another surgery. Minnie tried to keep it together but ultimately felt her heart race. The doctor continued to talk about the medical procedures before pulling out a needle.

Minnie immediately shut her eyes.

She realized that this was a remarkable tactic.

She kept her eyes shut until she heard the door fly open.

"Get out," Arthur impatiently said.

Minnie's eyes flew open. She was more than happy to oblige.

"What were you doing in there?" Arthur demanded.

"You said that I had to face my fears," Minnie quietly said, "You never said that I couldn't close my eyes."

Victor cheered.

Perry gave her a high-five.

Nicolas chuckled.

Arthur merely scowled.

Minnie didn't feel like waiting around to see the others' fears. She wheeled back up to her room, used the bathroom, and promptly collapsed. She had nightmares about hospitals, doctors, and infections...

Minnie jerked awake as someone touched her shoulder.

"Dinner," Victor gently said.

Minnie gasped as she realized what time it was.

She sat up and cried, "I didn't miss another challenge, did I?"

"No, no," Victor assuredly said, "This one took a lot longer than Arthur had expected. Some people had some really detailed fears."

He looked troubled for a moment.

Minnie quickly changed the subject by asking what was for dinner.

"The chefs set up several stations," Victor remarked, "I believe that there's a chicken station, a pasta station, and a vegetarian station."

"You do realize that this is basically a college fraternity?" Minnie teased.

Victor chuckled and said, "You're not that far off, actually. The Brotherhood of Merlin was created when Merlin started taking students in."

"Wait," Minnie suddenly said, "If Merlin treated you all like his children then why did you call yourselves his Brotherhood?"

"I've found that it's best not to question things,"

Victor retorted.

"Fair enough."

Minnie used the bathroom and followed Victor down to the dining hall. They gathered their food before joining Nicolas, Perry, and Miss Kiss.

The tension was thick as everyone thought about their projected fears.

Minnie finally broke it by asking, "Greatest historical moment that you've witnessed?"

"Who can choose?" Perry breathlessly asked.

"History has certainly been fun," Victor admitted.

Miss Kiss didn't even look up from her plate as she said, "Says the white guy."

Victor started to chuckle.

The laugh ultimately died off and was replaced by a small frown.

At long last, he muttered, "Good point."

He looked around before worriedly saying, "Where's Dmitri?"

"The zoo," Miss Kiss explained, "He went to see Firestone."

"Zoo?" Minnie repeated.

Victor grinned and said, "Do you want to see?"

Minnie eagerly nodded.

She followed Victor through the castle and out onto the grounds. He helped push her over the hills until they finally reached a large zoo. Minnie's jaw dropped.

"All of the magical animals within are going extinct," Victor admitted, "The Brotherhood takes them in and ensures that they're safe."

After seeing the unicorns yesterday, Minnie couldn't wait to see what other mystical creatures existed. She glanced at the first pen and was unable to suppress a scream.

A large monster was flying around. It was as if someone online had taken a picture of a lion, a picture of a dragon, and a picture of a goat before mashing them together. It was terrifying! Minnie tried to regulate her breathing.

"That's a chimaera," Victor calmly said, "Its name is Ashley."

"Ashley?"

Victor nodded.

He seemed completely nonplussed by the monster.

Minnie anxiously followed him to the second fenced-in area. She was quite sure that she was going to have a heart-attack. She was staring at a large lion with bat wings and a scorpion's tail. Victor claimed that it was a Manticore.

"What's its name?" Minnie squeaked.

"Bob."

Minnie noticed the entrance to the unicorn's grove. She hadn't realized that it was a part of a bizarre zoo. She wheeled over to the archway and peered in. She spotted several unicorns gracefully prancing around. Rainwater admiringly called her name and trotted over.

"Hey, Rainwater," Minnie whispered.

"Hello, Minerva Banks."

"Thanks for helping me out yesterday," Minnie gently said.

"You are welcome."

Minnie hesitated before adding, "I'm sorry for what Felix did."

"I do not blame Felix," Rainwater calmly said, "I blame Arthur."

Minnie gave a start and asked, "What do you mean?"

"Felix is nothing more than a small blaze," Rainwater explained, "Arthur is the one who fans the flames until they are out of control."

Minnie didn't want to contradict the noble unicorn. Yet she had a feeling that Felix would be a destructive fire with or without Arthur's presence.

"You are wrong," Rainwater simply said.

Minnie's cheeks reddened as she realized that Rainwater had read her thoughts. It would explain why the unicorns had been so quick to accept her answers yesterday; they could tell that she was telling the truth. Minnie briefly wondered if Perry visited the unicorns and had completely telepathic conversations with them.

"Yes," Rainwater chuckled, "Quite lovely conversations."

Minnie smiled but still said, "Felix is a complete jerk. He kidnapped my sister, he hid an embezzling scheme, he's committed a countless number of felonies, he pushed me down a flight of stairs...all within the past three months!"

"I am not excusing his actions," Rainwater replied, "I am simply saying that merely taking him down is not going to be enough."

Minnie slowly nodded.

"I must go," Rainwater added, "Farewell for now, Minerva Banks."

The unicorn trotted away, leaving a stunned Minnie in its wake.

She turned and saw that Victor looked extremely thoughtful.

At long last, the two continued on. They passed a large aquarium that was filled with beautiful mermaids and mermen. She stopped and stared at them in wonder. They gracefully swam around, twirling and somersaulting beneath the water. She was surprised at how many different body shapes there were. She was also surprised to see the different skin colors. A few of the mermaids noticed her and waved. Minnie awkwardly repeated the gesture.

Victor suddenly handed her a pair of thick, fluffy, earmuffs.

Minnie gave a start.

"Put them on," Victor commanded, "Don't take them off until I give you the gesture."

Minnie confusedly complied.

She followed Victor around the aquarium. They went beneath a beautiful glass archway that was filled with various types of strange fish. Minnie realized that the aquarium fed into a large pond. Several mermaid and mermen were sitting on large rocks. Their heads were thrown back and their mouths were wide open. An unexpected chill ran through Minnie's body.

It was a rather haunting scene.

She wheeled closer and could just make out the sound of a muffled song. The chilling melody caused Minnie to shiver once more. Yet, despite its eerie tone, it was also quite beautiful.

She needed to hear more!

Before Minnie knew what she was doing, she found herself reaching up and pulling the earmuffs from her ears. The song of the sirens seemed to hit her very bones. She could only gape at the large pond. She suddenly decided that this would be a very lovely day for a swim. The Brotherhood of Merlin didn't matter nor did New Quartz University. She was going to spend the rest of her life swimming with the mermaids and mermen. Never mind the fact that she *couldn't* swim. She was certain that she could learn. She was also certain that she could breathe underwater. There was only one way to find out...

Minnie jumped as two hands covered her own. They gently pushed the earmuffs back onto her ears. She looked up and saw that Victor was smirking down at her.

Minnie's face was on fire as she continued to follow him.

After a few minutes, Victor gave her a gesture.

Minnie removed her earmuffs.

Victor's smirk widened as he teasingly said, "Minerva Banks participates in class but refuses to follow directions."

"Sorry," Minnie mumbled.

Her cheeks were still warm.

"It's alright," Victor chuckled, "You aren't the first. The water was once up to my neck before Nicolas had the good grace to drag me out."

Minnie laughed.

"Come on," Victor added, "I want to show you Firestone."

"Who's Firestone?" Minnie apprehensively asked.

Victor merely jerked his head and walked on.

Minnie reluctantly followed him until they stopped outside a large pen.

Minnie squinted and saw yet another lion

hybrid. It was enormous! It was easily one of the largest animals in the 'zoo'. It was the size of an ambulance. Its head and front paws resembled a mighty lion yet its rear, hind legs, and wings resembled that of an eagle. Minnie realized that a very happy Dmitri was on the creature's back.

"Firestone," Victor proudly said.

"W...what is he?" Minnie stammered.

"A griffin," Victor explained, "Only with reversed ends. Most griffins have the front of an eagle and the rear of a lion."

Minnie realized that his purple eyes were sparkling as he stared at Firestone.

Upon noticing her stare, Victor flushed and said, "There was a time when Firestone and I were inseparable. I had to leave him behind when I was forced out of here."

He solemnly broke off.

Minnie wasn't sure what to say.

"Fortunately," Victor loudly continued, "Dmitri's taken good care of him."

Dmitri puffed out his chest.

He hopped off of the griffin and fell quite a ways before reaching the ground.

He picked himself up and cried, "Wanna pet him?"

Victor's eyes lit up.

He leapt right over the fence and raced over to

the griffin. Dmitri and Minnie both beamed as he tenderly stroked Firestone's mane. Firestone let out an affectionate growl.

"Well, go on," Dmitri cheerfully said, "Take him for a ride!"

Victor grinned at the thought.

He turned to Minnie.

"What?"

Victor's grin deepened into a smirk.

"No," Minnie cried, "No!"

The smirk widened.

Dmitri giggled.

"Don't you trust me?" Victor coyly asked.

Minnie shrugged and said, "It varies day-by-day."

Victor chuckled and stepped back over the fence.

"Come on," Victor whispered.

Minnie swallowed and nodded. Victor swooped his arm beneath her legs and gently picked her up. The golden light swirled around them. Dmitri continued to giggle.

"Shut up, kid," Victor muttered.

Dmitri merely smirked.

Victor stepped over the fence, floated up, and gently set Minnie on the griffin. She was right between his wings. Firestone was so large that she could sit with her legs crossed and still have plenty of room on the sides. She nervously clutched at its mixture of fur and feathers. Firestone let out a small rumble but was otherwise passive.

Victor leapt right on top of Firestone's head.

Minnie shook her head as his lower half was lost in the griffin's wild mane.

"Ready?" Victor called.

Minnie swallowed and nodded. Firestone's wings began to majestically flap. She screamed as he slowly flew up into the air. Minnie tightly closed her eyes and clung onto the griffin's fur/feathers so tightly that her knuckles hurt.

She could feel the breeze tug at her hair.

She could hear Victor whisper to Firestone.

From the way that the wind was increasing, Minnie deduced that they were flying higher and higher. All the more reason for her to keep her eyes shut.

Two gentle hands covered her fists.

Victor must have slid down Firestone's neck in order to kneel in front of her.

"Minerva," Victor gently said, "You're missing out on one heck of a view."

"I can imagine it," Minnie grunted.

Victor chuckled before carefully prying her fingers away from Firestone's fur/feathers. In turn, Minnie squeezed his hands. Victor squeezed right back.

"Open your eyes," Victor whispered, "Trust me."

Minnie reluctantly did so.

Victor's face swam into view.

His purple eyes were shining with tenderness and excitement. The wind was pulling at his ponytail and ruffling his shirt and vest. The golden light swirled around them.

"Look to your left," Victor coaxed.

Minnie did so and let out a staggering gasp.

Yet it was one of excitement.

The view was nothing less than breathtaking.

They were flying against a backdrop of intertwined hues of blue. Thousands of stars danced in her eyes. A large, round, moon was watching over them. Castle Tintagel was nothing more than a silhouette. Yet Minnie could see the golden light pouring out of the dozens of windows. A few clumps of white fluff floated past them. Minnie pulled away from Victor and reached out. One of the clouds practically melted at her touch. Minnie pulled her hand back and saw that it was covered with tiny droplets of water. Minnie beamed as she continued to take in the amazing view. She watched as a few of the stars shot across the sky.

Victor contently spread his arms out.

Minnie grinned and did the same.

Firestone slowly flew forward until it felt as though they were soaring against the heavens. Minnie flopped onto her stomach and Victor joined her. The two laid next to one another and looked at the sights.

"So," Victor softly said, "What do you think?"

"It's beautiful," Minnie gushed.

Victor smiled.

They continued to enjoy the view for a few more minutes.

Victor finally pushed himself onto his knees and suggested that Minnie do the same.

She complied and Victor added, "You might want to hold on."

"Why?"

He tapped Firestone's neck.

The griffin picked up speed.

Minnie nervously grabbed Victor's arm as Firestone abruptly dove. The golden light returned but neither one of them noticed. The ground drew closer and closer. Firestone pulled out of the dive and Minnie laughed as her stomach flipped.

The griffin did this again and again.

Minnie let out a whoop of joy and Victor laughed.

"Okay," Victor cried, "Now you're *really* going to want to hold on!"

The two clung onto Firestone as he began to twirl around. He weaved in and out of the clouds and flipped upside-down. Minnie let out an excited laugh. Victor held onto her so that she could throw her arms into the air. The griffin eventually turned right-side up once more. Victor instructed him to fly towards the castle.

They stopped outside a window and rapped on it.

Nicolas threw it open and could only stare at his brother and friend.

"Hey, Nicolas," Victor cheerfully said.

"Victor," Nicolas remarked, "Minerva."

Perry came to the window and laughed.

Victor extended his hand and asked, "Would you like a ride?"

"I'm good," Nicolas admitted.

Perry also declined the offer.

Nevertheless, they came out onto their balcony to watch as Victor and Minnie continued to soar through the air. Minnie's stomach continued to flip as Firestone did amazing stunts. She let out shouts from the deepest part her stomach; shouts that shook her entire body. Victor roared with laughter and excitement.

At long last, he steered Firestone back towards the zoo.

Dmitri happily ran over and met them on the ground.

Victor carried a flushed Minnie back to her wheelchair.

"Alright," Minnie gasped, "That was fun."

"See," Victor cried.

The three talked and laughed as they made their way back to the castle.

They ultimately quieted as they passed Arthur.

He looked absolutely furious.

The two went through the castle in silence. They reached their room and Victor ducked into the bathroom to take a shower. Minnie glanced up as Perry entered the room.

"So," Perry gently asked, "How was the ride?"

"It was amazing," Minnie gushed.

Perry beamed.

"Though Arthur sort of ruined the moment," Minnie added, "Why does he always get so mad whenever Victor and I are together?"

"He thinks that you two are madly in love," Perry simply said, "And that your love will ultimately cause you two to make bad decisions that will cause the world to crumble."

Minnie stared at her for a moment.

At long last, she muttered, "Huh..."

"Ignore Arthur," Perry continued, "Nothing that you do is going to make him happy. You might as well just..."

She hesitated as she thought of the right thing to say.

She finally smiled and said, "Enjoy the ride."

CHAPTER SEVEN

Rays of sunshine kissed Victor and Minnie as they strolled through the gardens. The wind tousled their hair. Several chirping birds flew past them.

The other members of the Brotherhood were also enjoying the beautiful morning. Even the sight of Arthur and Felix couldn't drain their spirits.

Victor bent down and swiped several roses from the dirt.

He handed them to Minnie.

She smiled and cried, "Oh, I love them!"

"I love *you*," Victor declared.

Minnie gasped before exclaiming, "I love you, too!"

Arthur angrily opened his mouth.

"You do?" Victor exclaimed, "Truly?"

"Truly, I do!"

Victor dropped down on one knee and gushed, "Then, Minerva Banks, would you make me the happiest man on earth?"

Arthur charged forward.

He was blocked by the other members of the Brotherhood. They were crowding around the two with smiles on their faces. Some were sniffing.

Minnie wiped her eyes and whispered, "Oh, Victor…"

She paused and asked, "Do you have a ring?"

Victor faltered and said, "I do not."

Perry took her wedding ring from her finger and handed it to Victor.

"I do," Victor cried, "I have a ring!"

"A ring from another girl?" Minnie wailed.

She clutched her chest and bit back a sob.

"She means nothing to me," Victor promised, "Nothing, I say."

He held the ring up and asked, "Minerva, will you marry me?"

"Oh, Victor," Minnie whispered, "Of course I will!"

The Brotherhood cheered.

Victor slipped the ring onto Minnie's finger before asking, "Is anyone here an ordained minister?"

Nicolas stepped forward and said, "I'm an ordained minister."

"Then marry us!" Victor ordered, "At once!"

"Certainly," Nicolas remarked, "Victor...?"

"I do."

"Minerva...?"

"I do."

"By the power vested in me by Merlin," Nicolas eloquently said, "I now pronounce you man and wife!"

"To our honeymoon!" Victor boomed.

Victor and Minnie roamed through the gardens

for several seconds.

"Wait," Victor abruptly said.

"What is it, my love?" Minnie asked.

Victor slowly turned away from her.

"Victor," Minnie exclaimed, "Darling, what is it?"

"I can't do this anymore, Minerva," Victor whispered, "I...I'm sorry."

"Victor, you can't!"

"I must!"

Victor began to walk away.

"But Victor," Minnie whined, "What of...the baby?"

The Brotherhood gasped.

Victor slowly turned and whispered, "You never mentioned..."

"I never had the chance," Minnie cried, "You were always at work."

"Damn it, Minerva," Victor whispered, "I worked so much so that I could provide for you! Because I love you."

"I love you, too!"

Victor turned around and croaked, "You do?"

"Of course, my love."

Victor stepped forward and whispered, "Tell me something..."

Minnie swallowed.

"The baby," Victor softly said, "Is it mine?"

Minnie hesitated.

Victor's jaw dropped.

"It doesn't matter," Minnie insisted, "I love you, now. Isn't that enough?"

Victor turned his head.

"Victor, please," Minnie pleaded, "Please..."

"When?"

"You were at work so much," Minnie explained, "I needed someone who could take care of me."

"But I can take care of you."

"I know that, now," Minnie agreed, "Oh, Victor..."

"If not me," Victor murmured, "Who?"

Minnie wistfully gazed at Nicolas.

"I should have known," Victor grumbled.

He unsheathed his sword.

"Victor, love," Minnie gasped, "Whatever are you doing?"

"I shall fight for you, my darling!"

"Wait," Nicolas spoke up, "What?"

He let out a yell as Victor promptly tackled him.

"Stop, stop!" Minnie shrieked, "Can't you see that this senseless violence is tearing us apart?"

"You must choose, Minnie," Victor declared, "Is it me or Nicolas?"

The two stood up.

Minnie let out a wail as she gazed back and forth.

"Choose!" Victor ordered.

"I choose Nicolas," Minnie blurted out.

"Ah," Nicolas quietly said, "But what you didn't realize was that I'm not really Nicolas! I am really...the King of Sweden."

The Brotherhood collectively gasped.

"You're right," Minnie admitted, "I didn't see that coming."

She turned to Victor and whispered, "Darling, don't you see? This changes everything! We can be together now!"

"No, we cannot."

"What do you mean?"

"I'm sorry, Minerva," Victor whispered, "I'm dying from a disease that I failed to tell you about."

He promptly collapsed.

"Victor," Minnie exclaimed, "NO!"

She fell from her wheelchair to weep next to him.

"Minerva?" Victor croaked.

"Victor," Minnie gasped, "You're alive!"

"Your tears brought me back to life," Victor explained.

The two embraced.

"I love you, Victor Flamel."

"I love you too, Minerva Banks."

The Brotherhood collectively cheered.

They all turned to face Arthur.

His face was beet red, his eye was twitching, and Minnie was sure that they had given him at least three heart-attacks.

At long last, he snarled, "Screw you guys."

"Hey, now," Minnie cried, "That'll make the wedding night more interesting."

Victor was the first to lose it.

Minnie joined him, as did Nicolas and Perry.

The rest of the Brotherhood quickly followed suit.

"Fantastic job, everyone," Victor commended, "If using our magic and wisdom to shape history doesn't work out, we can always start an improv group."

The Brotherhood continued to laugh.

A series of crackles and pops caused them to stop.

Arthur seemed to swell with rage.

"Was all of this simply to anger me?" Arthur dangerously asked.

Victor admittedly nodded.

"You looked like a bunch of idiotic fools!"

"Who cares?" Dmitri blurted out, "It was fun!"

"Fun?"

"Fun," Perry cried, "It's a feeling of enjoyment that you get from performing an activity. I imagine that you experience it when you torture us."

Arthur rolled his eyes before muttering, "You

still looked like childish fools!"

He was staring right at Victor.

"He said to the man who dressed up as Santa Claus," Minnie muttered.

She found herself smiling at the memory.

"What?" Victor snorted.

"You know," Minnie pressed, "That time that you dressed up as Santa Claus and entertained the children at New Quartz General?"

Victor stared at her for a moment before cheerfully saying, "Alright, Minerva's officially lost her mind! It was to be expected, really. I'm surprised that she held out for this long."

Minnie swatted him and said, "Very funny."

Victor was still looking at her as if she had sprouted an extra head.

"You don't have to deny it," Minnie pointed out, "I mean, it was incredibly silly but it was also really sweet."

Perry nodded and said, "Especially when you handed them toys from the gift shop."

Victor nudged Nicolas before muttering, "Minerva has dragged your wife into her world of nonsensical lunacy. That's fine. That's good. That's not concerning at all."

The women stared at him.

"He really doesn't remember," Perry finally said.

"Did you repress it?" Minnie laughed.

Victor shrugged and said, "I've repressed a lot of things."

He turned to Nicolas and asked, "Do *you* remember-?"

"No," Nicolas admitted, "However, I think that you gave me a concussion when you tackled me just now. Why the heck did you tackle me?"

"It made the Brotherhood laugh," Victor pointed out.

He proved his point by tackling Nicolas once more.

Sure enough, a majority of the Brotherhood erupted into giggles.

"Members of the Brotherhood of Merlin," Arthur boomed, "Have you become corrupted within just a few days? Have you forgotten who you're laughing alongside?"

Most of the members uncomfortably squirmed.

It was evident that they had.

The air continued to crackle and pop as Arthur glared at them.

"Go on," Arthur thundered, "Make a mockery out of my concerns. But when Victor ultimately brings your demise, just remember that your king tried to warn you!"

They continued to squirm like a bunch of guilty kindergarteners.

"Yes," Nicolas spoke up, "How dare you?"

He staggered to his feet and pulled Victor up alongside him.

"How dare you experience a moment of frivolity?" Nicolas asked, "How dare you experience a moment of happiness? How dare you experience a positive interaction with my brother? How dare you not shun him? How dare you not kick and curse him? How dare a few of you even show some forgiveness? How dare you show anything other than sixteen-hundred-years of pent-up rage and resentment?"

The tension had substantially waned.

A few people were even cracking smiles.

For a moment, Arthur and Nicolas merely stared at one another.

One was shaking with fury.

The other was calm and collected.

The former spun on his heel and stomped away.

Minnie let out a low whistle.

She had never seen anyone with so much hatred towards one person. The Brotherhood disbanded until Victor and Minnie were the only ones in the garden.

"Alright," Minnie eventually said, "I have two questions."

Victor grinned and said, "Don't worry; Nicolas isn't really an ordained minister."

"Thank God," Minnie laughed, "But that wasn't one of them."

"Fire away."

"Why aren't you dead?" Minnie asked.

Victor snorted and said, "What?"

"Arthur clearly hates you," Minnie pointed out, "And he's worked hard to get the other members of the Brotherhood to hate you as well. Why haven't they tried to execute you?"

"Oh, they wanted to," Victor replied, "And they nearly came close."

A shadow crossed his face.

"What stopped them?" Minnie whispered.

Victor hesitated before saying, "What's your second question?"

"Why isn't Nicolas the king?" Minnie asked, "He seems much more qualified than Arthur. He'd be a great king!"

"Yes," Victor sadly said, "He would."

Minnie waited for a moment before prompting, "So...?"

"Your second question answers your first," Victor declared.

Minnie rolled her eyes and muttered, "Is it possible for you to ever give someone a straightforward answer?"

Victor stared at her for a moment before walking away.

"Yeah," Minnie sighed, "I saw that one coming."

Victor soon returned with a dusty book. He gingerly flipped through it before finding the page that he wanted. He showed it to Minnie. Her brow furrowed as she read the excerpt:

And thus the deal wast made.
He relinquished the Crown.
To spare the Life.
He relinquished the Sword.
To spare the Brothership.
And thus the sacrifice wast made.

"Okay," Minnie slowly said, "What does that mean?"

She looked up and was shocked to find that Victor's purple eyes were watery.

"It means," Victor whispered, "That my brother is a great man."

A cold gust of air caused the two to shiver.

"Come on," Victor softly said, "Let's get back up to the castle."

Minnie nodded and followed him. Her mind was still buzzing as she tried to comprehend the excerpt from the book. She didn't know what it meant but she knew that Victor was tremendously affected by it. She glanced over a few times and saw that he was swallowing lumps in his throat. She opened her mouth but didn't know what to say.

They proceeded to the dungeons in silence.

They joined the rest of the group.

"Oh, there you are," Perry cried, "The next challenge is getting out of a locked room."

"It should be fairly simple," Nicolas mumbled, "Especially for an inventor."

He smiled but his brother didn't return it.

"Are you alright?" Nicolas asked.

Victor sighed and mumbled, "I'm sorry."

"For what?" Nicolas chuckled, "The tackle out there. You should be! I don't mind playing along with you and Minerva but I would rather not break my hip..."

He trailed off as he realized that Victor wasn't paying attention.

"Minerva," Arthur abruptly said, "Enter the chamber."

Minnie gave Victor a final glance before doing so.

She jumped as the door crashed shut.

She glanced around the room.

Several tables were covered with various magical tools. Minnie knew that they were useless to her as she had no idea how to use them. The last thing she wanted was to pick up the wrong tool and set the entire castle on fire. Minnie honestly had no idea what to do.

She gazed through the window and watched as Victor gave her a weak smile.

Minnie thought of the first day that they had met. Victor had shown her the stars. The two had been on a hill across from New Quartz General

Hospital. They had bonded and Minnie had promptly stabbed him in the back. At least he didn't hold a grudge!

Minnie's eyes widened as she remembered just how she had stabbed him in the back.

She suddenly had an idea!

Minnie took a deep breath and shifted her weight. The wheelchair ended up tipping sideways and she crashed to the ground. Minnie screamed in pain before becoming limp.

She could hear shouts from the other side of the wall.

After a few moments, Arthur wrenched the door open and snapped, "What is wrong with you, Minerva?"

"Nothing," Minnie cheerfully said.

She pushed herself up onto her knees and continued, "Thanks for opening the door!"

Arthur spluttered.

Minnie hummed a happy tune as she pushed her wheelchair back into the right position and climbed up into it. She wheeled past a horrified Arthur and was immediately surrounded by her friends. Victor was incoherently screaming with joy. Perry, Dmitri, and Miss Kiss took turns tightly hugging her. Nicolas patted her shoulder and congratulated her.

"No!" Arthur finally howled, "That's not fair!"

"It's absolutely fair," Nicolas remarked.

"She keeps cheating!" Arthur exclaimed.

"She's not cheating," Nicolas simply said, "She is merely following one of Merlin's oldest philosophies."

"And what's that?"

Nicolas smiled and said, "Opening your mind to the possibilities."

CHAPTER EIGHT

Minnie's eyelids were heavy.

She let her head fall onto Victor's shoulder.

The golden light swirled around them, causing Minnie to squint.

Victor chuckled before grabbing the cushion from Minnie's wheelchair. He placed it between her head and his shoulder. Minnie sleepily thanked him.

The two were sitting on a couch in a large lounge. Most of the Brotherhood was squashed into the room. Nicolas was stoking the flames in a stone fireplace. Hot tea and hot cocoa were being passed around. Stories were being told. Minnie noted that the only absent members were Arthur and Gwen. The cloaked Knights were sitting in one corner. Felix was awkwardly sitting between them and the other members of The Quartet.

"Tired, Minerva?" Felix called, "It's not easy playing with the big kids, is it?"

"Shut up," Minnie mumbled.

Speaking of tired...

A thought occurred to her.

"Hey," Minnie spoke up, "Where do you sleep?"

Felix raised his eyebrows before saying, "My bedroom."

"Your what?"

"My bedroom," Felix repeated, "It's a room with a bed in it."

It took Minnie a moment to realize what he was saying.

"You...you live here?" Minnie stammered.

"Why wouldn't I?" Felix retorted, "Unlike some people, *I* wasn't exiled."

He pointedly glanced at his brothers and sister-in-law.

"That's a shame," Victor admitted, "It's pretty much become a family tradition at this point."

A few members of the Brotherhood laughed.

Minnie was still stuck on the fact that Felix lived here.

She glanced at Christopher, Thomas, and Theodore and asked, "Do you live here, too?"

They nodded.

"Then why do you come to New Quartz City?" Minnie blurted out.

She straightened herself up and the wheelchair cushion fell to the floor.

"You're the city's self-proclaimed superheroes," Minnie cried, "You've been there almost every night since I first moved in with Victor. Do you literally travel across a giant ocean just to mess with your brother?"

Felix exchanged strange looks with the other members of The Quartet.

Miss Kiss changed the subject before the villains could answer.

"Did you say that you moved in with Victor?" Miss Kiss exclaimed.

Whispers swept throughout the room.

Minnie and Victor nodded.

Miss Kiss smirked before saying, "The two of you are living together, Victor gave you the pin, the golden light occurs whenever you touch..."

"Just say it," Minnie sighed, "Everyone else has."

She was confident that she was prepared for whatever Miss Kiss was going to say.

"So when are you going to dump honey on his head?"

Minnie gave a start.

She wasn't even remotely prepared for that.

She realized that Miss Kiss was staring at Nicolas.

Several people laughed, including the alchemist.

"When he least expects it," Nicolas finally said.

Victor smirked and said, "I dare you."

"Okay, what?" Minnie laughed.

Victor's smirk widened as he said, "One day, when Felix and I were innocent children, we decided that we would help our brother woo a young woman."

"Naturally," Felix agreed, "Nicolas didn't see it that way, of course, but we truly had his best interest at heart."

"You two flew up behind me and dumped honey all over my head," Nicolas exclaimed.

"In order to help you," Victor patiently said.

"Again," Felix added, "We only had your best interest at heart."

He and Victor exchanged glances before snickering.

They both seemed to realize who the other one was for they quickly composed themselves. Minnie was caught between laughing and frowning. On the one hand, the thought of Nicolas having honey in his hair was hilarious! On the other hand, it still made her uncomfortable when Victor and Felix acted civil towards one another.

She pushed the discomfort away and asked, "So, who was the lucky woman?"

Perry's smirk said it all.

She gave a blushing Nicolas a peck on the cheek.

"Can we please change the subject?" Nicolas asked.

Minnie was kind enough to oblige by saying, "So, where's the round table?"

"Oh, Arthur got rid of that centuries ago," Victor briskly said, "He traded it in for a throne-room wherein he's the only one permitted to sit. At least, until you showed up."

"Has he always been a bigoted jerk?" Minnie asked.

"Pretty much," Nicolas admitted, "Though it definitely increased after-"

He caught Victor's eye and ultimately hushed.

Minnie noticed that Felix's face had hardened.

This brought her back to the earlier topic.

"How do you get to New Quartz City?" Minnie wondered, " And how do you get back here?"

"That's for us to know," Felix mysteriously said.

Minnie rolled her eyes before crying, "Okay, I have one last question for you."

"Why stop now?"

"Why do you even pretend to be a superhero?" Minnie cried, "I'm sure that there are other glorious ways that you can mess with your brother."

"I do those as well," Felix admitted, "Surely Victor has told you that we blend into the current trends of the times? It's traditional."

"Yeah," Minnie muttered, "Sure."

It still made no sense to her.

"The world doesn't make any sense, remember?" Perry whispered.

"So," Dmitri spoke up, "How'd you and Victor meet?"

Minnie and Victor respectively spoke:

"He crashed through the ceiling at the store."

"She offered to help Felix."

"Felix refused my offer."

"She hit me in the head with her footrest."

Minnie chuckled; she had almost forgotten about that!

She continued, "Thomas and Theodore sent me to New Quartz General on a 'mission'."

"I showed her the stars."

"You did?" Miss Kiss gasped.

"He did, indeed," Perry warmly said.

The two grinned at one another.

"Anyway," Victor loudly said, "Minerva betrayed me."

"Then I made the biggest mistake of my life."

"Then she threw hot coffee and hot tea at The Quartet."

"Then Victor said that the glowing light meant that our destinies were intertwined.

"Aw, Victor," Miss Kiss spoke up, "You beautiful little liar, you."

Victor glared at her before saying, "Our destinies *were* intertwined."

"Nicolas and Perry eventually stopped by," Minnie continued, "Some weird things happened. I ultimately realized that Felix and The Quartet were corrupt assholes, though that still didn't stop Victor from inviting his brother to Christmas dinner."

She couldn't keep the bitterness out of her tone as she said the last part.

Victor's eyebrows raised.

"Hey, wait a minute!" Minnie abruptly said,

"How are you guys alive?"

Miss Kiss gave a start before saying, "We're immortal."

"Well, yes," Minnie cried, "I figured that much out on my own. *How* are you all immortal? Did Nicolas and Perry make Elixirs for all of you?"

"We would have," Perry admitted, "Well, most of you."

Her reply was met with chuckles and giggles.

"Arthur found his own means of immortality and was nice enough to share it with the rest of the Brotherhood," Nicolas explained, "Felix, Victor, Dmitri, Perenelle, and I are the only ones who use the Elixir of Life."

Minnie accepted this answer.

"So, go on," Dmitri prompted, "What happened after you found out that Felix was a corrupt as-"

"Don't finish that sentence," Victor warned.

Minnie smiled before saying, "I moved in with Victor and became an Antagonist."

Several people gasped.

"You...what?" Miss Kiss exclaimed.

Minnie gave a start before saying, "I became an Antag-"

"Don't say it again," Miss Kiss cried, "Why would you do such a thing?"

"She's not *really* an Antagonist," Victor spoke up, "She's just being smart."

Several people relaxed.

"Minerva," Miss Kiss eventually said, "You *never* want to call yourself an Antagonist. Antagonists are cruel, vile, evil..."

"Hey," Victor interjected, "I've done alright."

Someone spoke up, "You literally led to the death of our leader."

"Other than that," Victor hastily said.

Some people chuckled, others looked troubled.

"I don't get it," Minnie cried, "It's a *word*."

"It's not just a word," Miss Kiss argued, "It's a part of an ancient prophecy-"

"Well maybe the prophecy's wrong," Minnie declared.

The Flamels were the only ones who didn't look shocked.

"Felix is a Protagonist," Minnie pointed out, "And he's done some really terrible things. Victor's an Antagonist and he's done some great things! Who says that the prophecy is right? Who says that you have to follow it?"

"That's outrageous!"

"Asinine!"

"Unthinkable!"

Minnie sighed as she realized that she wasn't getting anywhere.

She ultimately dropped the topic but secretly decided that she was still going to call herself an

Antagonist. If Victor couldn't change his title then she wasn't going to change hers.

"Leave it to a mortal to not understand a prophecy."

Everyone turned and saw that Arthur had entered the room.

Minnie flinched at the way that he said 'mortal'.

She ultimately pulled herself together and said, "So, the gender, age, skin color, and disability aren't what you're judging? It's the fact that I'm mortal? Alright then..."

Victor chuckled.

"There are only a handful of mortals who are worthy enough to be around the likes of us," Arthur declared, "You are not one of them."

"Good to know," Minnie sarcastically said.

She saw that Felix was nodding along with Arthur's jeers.

A wave of white hot fury washed over her.

She grabbed her cushion and threw it onto her chair. She quickly transferred into it before tapping her scabbard thrice.

"I'll show you who's worthy," Minnie growled.

"Minerva," Victor cried, "Don't!"

Minnie froze as Arthur withdrew Excalibur from its sheath.

There was a blur as someone leapt in front of her. Minnie was about to push Victor aside when she realized that it wasn't Victor at all.

It was Nicolas.

"It's been a long day," Nicolas quietly said, "I suggest that we all go to bed."

There was a moment's pause before everyone reluctantly complied.

Minnie's chest rose and fell as she made her way back to her room.

Victor, Nicolas, and Perry followed her.

"Perhaps I forgot to mention," Victor cried, "You *never* want to challenge R. There's only one member of the entire Brotherhood who has ever bested him."

"You *did* forget to mention that," Minnie remarked, "Then again, you also forgot that you dressed up as Santa so..."

"Okay," Victor muttered, "Minerva's losing her mind again."

"Victor," Perry spoke up, "What do you remember about that day?"

"I woke up," Victor explained, "I made breakfast. Minerva came down. We ate together. You and Nicolas arrived. Felix took Elizabeth as collateral. Minerva made a great speech before defeating Felix. I showed you the skyline of New Quartz City."

"That's all well and good," Perry cried, "However, what do you remember about the middle of the day?"

Victor opened his mouth before shutting it

again.

"I want to try something," Perry muttered.

She followed Victor and Minnie into their bedroom. She then instructed Victor to lie down on the bed. Victor raised his eyebrows before doing so.

Perry lifted her arms and he let out a loud scream.

"Sorry," Perry apologetically said, "I'll try to be gentle..."

Yet another scream told her that her attempts were fruitless.

"What are you trying to do?" Victor gasped, "Rip my brain apart?"

"I'm sorry," Perry cried, "I'm just trying to help you remember."

"You really don't remember anything else about that day?" Minnie asked.

It was one of the most prominent days in her own memory.

Victor sat up and rubbed his temple.

At long last, he mumbled, "I remember...Kellington...Felix..."

He frustratedly broke off.

"Speaking of Kellington."

Nicolas entered the room.

Minnie's heart sank as she realized that he looked grim.

"I was just checking the news on my phone,"

Nicolas softly said, "Gregory Kellington has escaped from prison."

CHAPTER NINE

Minnie hadn't gotten any sleep.

She had spent the night thinking about Kellington.

The news app had said that Kellington had escaped several days ago. The police had no leads.

Minnie had spent the entire morning growing angrier and angrier.

She barely paid attention as Arthur gestured to the large circle that he had made in the middle of the chamber. She couldn't care less as he made the announcement that the next challenge would be a swordfight in which one member challenged another.

Her only priority was Kellington.

The past few days had been so busy that Minnie had completely forgotten about him. Now he was all that she could think about. Minnie took a deep breath and tried to focus on what Arthur was saying. Yet her eye was drawn to Felix. He was talking with the other members of The Quartet. They glanced around before slinking away.

Minnie hesitated before following them.

She wasn't aware of the fact that Victor was following her.

"HEY!"

Minnie's roar rang throughout the corridor.

Felix, Christopher, Thomas, and Theodore all turned.

"WHERE'S KELLINGTON?" Minnie demanded, "WHERE IS HE?"

Felix's mouth curved into a smirk.

"What makes you think that I know?" Felix teased.

Minnie clenched her fists and growled, "Do you?"

"Of course."

Minnie tapped her scabbard and withdrew her sword.

Felix threw his head back and cackled.

"Do you really think that you can intimidate me?" Felix spat, "You truly are the world's biggest retard."

"And you are the world's biggest jerk," Minnie retorted, "I can take the four of you."

Felix's smirk deepened and he snarled, "You just don't get it, do you?"

Minnie blinked.

Felix suddenly had a twin.

She blinked again.

There were triplets.

It wasn't long before Minnie was completely surrounded by Felix and his 'clones'. They laughed and shouted out insults.

Her skin crawled as his voice chorused, "Don't

you get it? I can become anyone! I can become anything!"

Minnie shook with anger.

Before she knew what she was doing, she had pulled out her sword. The blade sliced through one of the many clones. She watched as it was reduced to nothing more than a puddle.

Another clone quickly took its place.

Minnie swung again and again.

She was aware of the fact that a crowd had formed but she didn't care.

She continued to swing at the clones until she nearly took Victor's head off. She gave a start and he used the opportunity to swiftly disarm her.

Minnie glared at him as her chest rapidly rose and fell.

"Take it easy, Minerva," Victor gently said, "Breathe...breathe..."

"For God's sake, Victor," Perry chastised, "She's not going into labor!"

She hit Victor's arm before adding, "Are you okay, Minnie?"

Minnie shook her head.

Felix and his clones roared with laughter.

"Knock it off," Nicolas sharply said.

There was a moment's pause before Felix reluctantly complied. The clones disappeared until there was just one smirking jerk. He still continued to chortle. Several members of the Brotherhood joined in, including Arthur.

Minnie's blood was boiling.

She clenched her fists and locked her jaw. It was one of the few times in her life when she was visibly shaking with anger. Perry apprehensively called her name.

Minnie reached into her backpack and grabbed the first thing that her fingers hit – her hairbrush. She threw it as hard as she could. It hit the back of Felix's head, causing him to spin around in alarm. Victor, Perry, and Nicolas exchanged stunned glances.

"I challenge Felix," Minnie feverishly said.

"You what?" Victor cried.

Felix threw his head back and laughed.

Nicolas grabbed her shoulder and whispered, "You don't want to do this."

Minnie wrenched away and growled, "I absolutely want to do this!"

"You won't want the consequences of doing this," Nicolas exasperatedly clarified.

"Minerva," Victor whispered, "Please..."

"It's not going to end well," Perry pressed.

Minnie stared at them in disbelief.

They really didn't think that she could take him.

"It's not that," Perry gently said, "It's just—"

Minnie didn't hear the rest. Felix had stepped forward and had accepted the duel. He stepped into the circle. Minnie took a deep breath and wheeled in.

A crowd quickly formed. Victor, Nicolas, and Perry were anxiously holding onto one another. That did little to comfort Minnie.

"At least wear your armor," Victor pressed.

Minnie sighed and gave in.

She squeezed her bracelet and watched as the armor spread across her body. She then tapped her scabbard and caused it to appear. Minnie pulled out her sword and held it up.

Felix did the same.

A very amused Arthur stepped forward and boomed, "BEGIN!"

The two raced towards one another.

Felix abruptly grabbed the handle of her wheelchair and spun her around. Minnie cried out but it was too late. Despite her throwing on the brakes, the corrupt jerk was still able to push her out of the circle. He even tipped the chair so that she ended up falling out.

Her face burned at the loud laughs.

"Minerva?"

Victor, Nicolas, and Perry crouched down next to her.

"He cheated," Minnie spat, "The bastard cheated!"

"Imagine that," Victor retorted, "*Felix* cheated."

He was trying to look sympathetic.

Yet his eyes were blazing as he asked, "You're lucky that you weren't killed. What were you thinking?"

"I was thinking that I wanted to wipe that smirk off of your brother's face," Minnie growled, "I would have done just that if he hadn't played dirty."

"That's what Felix does," Nicolas patiently said.

That didn't remotely help.

"Minerva," Victor softly said, "You can't let him get to you."

"It's hard not to," Minnie argued, "He's always—"

"We know," Perry interrupted, "We know how much of a pain he is. We've lived with him for sixteen-hundred years. Believe me, we know."

Minnie spoke through clenched teeth, "In that case, how can you guys possibly justify telling me to change myself around him?"

"We're not," Perry replied, "You're normally very level-headed. I'm telling you to stay that way. No matter how much he tries to bait you, just remain calm."

"Otherwise," Nicolas spoke up, "You're giving him exactly what he wants."

Victor nodded and said, "It's best to just remain civil around him."

Something in Minnie snapped.

Her neck ached as she quickly turned towards

him.

Victor seemed to sense that something was off for he leaned backwards.

"Fine," Minnie hissed, "I'll remain civil. Maybe I'll even invite him to Christmas dinner!"

She climbed into her wheelchair and left without another word.

She could hear Victor, Perry, and Nicolas respectively whisper behind her.

"What was that about?"

"Victor, she's been upset about that for months."

"You honestly haven't noticed?"

Minnie turned the corner and was out of earshot.

She wheeled back up to her room and went out onto the balcony. Her entire body ached but she was too upset to even notice. She leaned against the railing and stared out at the grounds.

Her stomach twisted as Victor come out.

"Hello," Victor awkwardly said.

"Hey," Minnie bit.

Victor hesitated before saying, "Perenelle and Nicolas have informed me that you were upset about my decision to invite Felix to Christmas dinner a few months ago."

"Always observant, those two."

"Why didn't you say anything at the time?"

Minnie's teeth were clenched as she said, "I tried but you insisted that he was your brother."

Victor shrugged and said, "Well, he *is*."

"Yeah."

Her tone was short and clipped.

Victor looked annoyed.

Minnie honestly didn't care.

Victor stuffed his hands in his pockets and was silent for a moment.

"If it helps," Victor eventually said, "You *would* have defeated Felix earlier. Just imagine the look on R's face. He would have had an aneurism!"

"Mm," Minnie muttered, "Maybe you should invite Arthur to Christmas dinner."

"Why are you so fixated on that?" Victor cried.

"Because," Minnie burst out, "Somebody has to point out how ridiculous it was! Felix had just tried to kill us and you invited him over. He had kidnapped Lizzie and you thought that it was okay to just let him sit at the same table as her. Do you realize how creepy that is?"

"I know," Victor sighed, "But—"

"But what?"

Victor gripped the railing and muttered, "At the end of the day, no matter what he's done, he's still my brother."

Minnie was silent for a moment.

She finally wheeled towards him and whispered,

"No, he's not."

Victor looked aghast.

"He might have been," Minnie softly said, "But the brotherly relationship that existed between you and Felix clearly ended the day that Merlin died. And no matter what you try to do, no matter how much you try to act like everything is normal, you're never going to be able to get that relationship back. Felix doesn't see you as his brother. He doesn't love you. He doesn't even like you! He hates you, he outright admits that he hates you, and he spends his days making sure that everyone else hates you. You need to stop seeing him as your brother and start seeing him as the self-righteous asshole that he is!"

Every emotion had crossed Victor's face until it was completely blank.

He turned away from her and cried, "You know, for someone who wants to be a psychologist, you sure have a way of telling people exactly what they don't want to hear."

"My job wouldn't be to tell people what they want to hear," Minnie retorted, "It would be to tell people what they need to hear."

Their voices had substantially risen.

"You think that I needed to hear that?"

"Yes."

Victor scoffed.

"I know that it's hard," Minnie continued, "But

you need to understand that your view of Felix is incredibly toxic."

"*Mine's* incredibly toxic?"

"Yeah!"

"You're the one who is always spitting fire whenever he's around!"

"BECAUSE HE'S FREQUENTLY TRYING TO KILL US!"

"AND FROM THE WAY THAT YOU'RE ALWAYS TALKING ABOUT HIM," Victor shouted, "I'M STARTING TO WONDER IF YOU WANT *HIM* DEAD!"

"WELL, I WOULD SAY 'THROW HIM IN PRISON,'" Minnie screamed, "BUT THEN HE MIGHT BEFRIEND A BUNCH OF CONVICTED MURDERERS AND YOU'LL INVITE THEM ALL OVER FOR SUNDAY BRUNCH!"

"Both of you need to stop!"

Victor and Minnie whirled around.

Nicolas and Perry were standing behind them.

The former had spoken.

"Everyone in the castle can hear you," Perry declared.

"Then help us settle the argument," Victor growled, "Which one of us is right?"

"Neither of you," Nicolas simply said.

Perry nodded in agreement.

Victor rolled his eyes and stomped back into the room.

He slammed the door so hard that the glass

cracked.

Nicolas and Perry exchanged solemn glances before doing something rather remarkable – they played a quick game of rock-paper-scissors. Perry lost and stomped away to comfort her brother-in-law. Nicolas stayed behind to talk to Minnie.

She buried her face in her hands.

She was aware of the fact that this had been the first true fight between her and Victor.

She was aware of the fact that she was heavily breathing.

She was aware of the fact that her eyes were stinging.

She was aware of the fact that Nicolas was staring at her.

"Are you alright?" Nicolas gently asked.

"Sure," Minnie muttered.

Nicolas chuckled and said, "I might not have my wife's telepathic powers but something tells me that you're lying."

Minnie looked up and growled, "It's just...frustrating..."

"I know," Nicolas gently said, "Take a few deep breaths."

Minnie did so before saying, "Victor's an intelligent man. I have no idea how he can possibly like Felix."

"Oh, he doesn't," Nicolas quickly said, "He hates

Felix as much as you do; possibly even more. However, there's still a part of him that remains hopeful. You see, everything changed on the night that Merlin died. Everything. By now, I'm sure that you've realized that Victor is the reason that such events occurred. He subsequently copes by trying to pretend that things can return to the way that they were before."

Minnie sighed and whispered, "What do you think?"

"I think that things will never be quite the same," Nicolas admitted, "However, I also think that my brother has gone through life with little hope. I know that I'm not going to be the one responsible for taking it away."

Minnie felt a pang of guilt.

"Are you going to tell me that I should play nice around Felix?" Minnie finally asked.

"Actually, I *was* going to tell you that," Nicolas softly said, "Not for Victor's sake but for yours. It's not healthy to have such negative emotions."

"Nicolas, look at me," Minnie laughed, "Nothing about me is healthy!"

Nicolas chuckled.

"Look," Minnie seriously continued, "I respect the fact that you're a pacifist—"

"Merlin was one as well."

"Yeah," Minnie muttered, "Well, I'm not

Merlin."

"True," Nicolas agreed, "However, you *are* joining his Brotherhood."

"I'm starting to wonder if that's such a good thing," Minnie softly said.

"It is."

Nicolas' reply was immediate.

"I thought that the Brotherhood was something great," Minnie explained, "I thought that it was something to be proud of. It's just a bunch of corrupt jerks who are using their power to keep being corrupt jerks."

"Not all of us our jerks," Nicolas pointed out, "I'd say that it's about evenly split."

"Because that's a lot better," Minnie sardonically said, "That's like saying that not *all* of the room is on fire; just half of it."

"A momentous difference if you're the one with the extinguisher," Nicolas replied.

"And how am I supposed to fight the flames when you want me to be a pacifist?"

"I just told you," Nicolas patiently said, "Use an extinguisher. Right now, your method is to fight the flames with more flames. That's just going to create a bigger fire."

Minnie wasn't really interested in pretentious metaphors; she was too tired – physically, mentally, and emotionally.

"You need to find other means to subdue Felix," Nicolas explained, "Trust me when I say that the non-violent response can sting just as much as the swing of a sword."

Minnie reluctantly nodded.

Nicolas checked his pocket-watch before saying, "You should get some rest."

He left and Minnie reluctantly entered the empty bedroom. She used the bathroom, changed into her pajamas, and flopped onto her bed. She was unable to get to sleep.

Yet she quickly feigned snoring as Victor entered the room.

Victor paused before saying, "You don't snore."

Minnie sighed. She still refused to roll over. Her eyes were stinging once more and something was stuck in her throat. She could hear Victor trying to apologize. She grunted and occasionally nodded, hoping that he would go away.

The last thing that she wanted was for him to see her like this.

Which is exactly why her heart sank when he whispered, "Hey, are you alright?"

"No," Minnie hoarsely admitted.

"Minerva..."

Victor hesitantly touched her shoulder.

Minnie crumbled. Hot tears fell down her face and bled into her pillow. Her entire body shook as she ashamedly cried.

"Hey, hey," Victor gently said, "It's alright."

When Minnie didn't answer, he spun around and raced away.

The bizarre action caused Minnie to finally turn and sit up.

Victor returned with Nicolas and Perry at his heels.

"They're here to make sure that I don't say something stupid," Victor admitted.

Minnie weakly chuckled.

In the end, Victor didn't say anything at all.

Neither did Perry.

Nor Nicolas.

They didn't need to.

Perry sat on one side of her and Victor sat on the other. Nicolas sat next to Victor. The four held one another until they weren't sure whose tears belonged to whom. There was no need to ask why they were upset. It had been a remarkably long day. It had been a remarkably long week. It had been a remarkably long couple of months. It had been a remarkably long life!

And so, the four held one another, seeking comfort from each other.

The last thing that Minnie saw before she drifted to sleep was that strange golden light that intertwined her and Victor.

CHAPTER TEN

Minnie couldn't remember a time when she had gotten such a great night of sleep.

She had even slept in.

Unfortunately, this resulted in her rushing around in order to get ready. She finally caught up with Victor, just as he was entering the dining hall.

"Are you okay?" Victor immediately asked.

"Fine," Minnie mumbled.

She noted that Victor looked incredibly thoughtful.

"What are you thinking about?" Minnie teased.

"How powerful my brother is," Victor admitted.

Minnie's shoulders sagged.

"My brother is a very powerful man," Victor quietly said, "He holds the world in his hands and he could crush it at any moment. He can make entire mountains crumble. He can make entire seas rise. He can control the sun, moon, and stars. He can make the entire universe bow at his will."

Victor finally broke off.

Minnie could only stare at him in wonder.

At long last, she whispered, "Wow..."

He rubbed the back of his neck but didn't take any of it back.

"I never knew that you thought that way about

Felix," Minnie admitted.

Victor gave a start and cried, "I'm not talking about Felix."

"Then, who...?"

"Nicolas, of course!"

It was Minnie's turn to give a start.

"Nicolas Flamel," Minnie slowly said, "The pacifist who spends his free-time drinking tea and playing the violin? He's the most powerful man in the universe?"

Victor nodded.

Minnie laughed before realizing that Victor was sincere.

She still remained skeptical.

"I'm not the only one who thinks so," Victor added, "Watch this."

The two entered the large dining hall.

They spotted Dmitri at the omelet station.

"Hey, Dmitri," Victor cried, "Who's the most powerful man in the universe?"

The seven-year-old immediately answered, "Nicolas."

Perry walked over and asked, "What about my husband?"

"Is he the most powerful man in the universe?" Victor asked.

"Without a doubt," Perry firmly said.

Minnie still wasn't convinced.

Victor reached out and grabbed the elbow of the passerby.

"Good morning, Felix," Victor exclaimed.

"What do you want?" Felix snapped.

"An answer to my question," Victor remarked, "Who is the most powerful man in the universe?"

"Our brother."

Felix's reply was instant.

He looked shocked that Victor was even asking such a question.

"Oh, come on!" Minnie laughed, "Nicolas wouldn't hurt a fly."

"That doesn't mean that he couldn't," Victor quietly said, "Merlin used to say that the greatest power in the universe was the ability to show restraint."

Felix nodded and reluctantly said, "As much as I hate to admit it, our brother's power knows no bounds. It's terrifying, really."

Perry beamed.

Minnie shook her head and mumbled, "I'm sorry but I really don't see myself ever being afraid of Nicolas."

"You should be."

It was the only time that Victor and Felix had ever spoken in unison.

"Listen to me, Minerva Banks," Felix

snarled, "Crossing me would be a very big mistake. Crossing King Arthur would be an even bigger one. But may Merlin's Spirit help you if you ever dare to cross Nicolas Flamel."

At that moment, Arthur entered the dining hall.

Felix immediately stepped away from Victor.

Arthur didn't even notice and instead instructed everyone to follow him to the dungeons.

They all complied and were shocked when Arthur ushered them into the same chamber as yesterday.

"It seems that Victor got into a bit of a fight last night," Arthur coyly said.

Victor and Minnie both flushed.

"However," Arthur continued, "Victor was not able to challenge anyone to a duel. I am ordering him to do so now."

Victor hesitated.

He finally stepped forward and said, "I challenge Arthur."

There was a chorus of gasps.

"Let me finish," Victor cried, "I challenge Arthur to duel Nicolas!"

The chorus of gasps rang out once more.

"What are you doing?" Nicolas whispered.

"I'm challenging Arthur to duel you," Victor cheerfully said.

Arthur roared with laughter before saying, "I

accept."

"King Arthur," Felix hissed, "I urge you to reconsider this."

Arthur merely pulled out Excalibur.

Nicolas borrowed Victor's sword.

The two men stepped into the circle.

Arthur's blows were swift, direct, and fierce.

Nicolas had crashed to the floor within minutes.

Minnie's hands flew to her mouth.

She could see the dismay on everyone else's faces.

Arthur's laugh shook the windows.

"Come on," Victor whispered, "Come on, Nicolas."

Nicolas lifted his head before lying down once more.

Felix had stopped pacing, coincidentally standing right next to Victor.

Arthur turned to them and sneered, "I have to give you credit, Victor. I thought that your brother would fall within the first minute! Yet, he managed to last a minute and a half."

Victor merely glared at him.

The members of the Brotherhood who were loyal to Arthur laughed.

All of them, that is, except for Felix.

His glare wasn't as intense as Victor's but it *was* prominent.

"Did you really think that Nicolas could defeat me?" Arthur thundered, "Passive, pathetic, Nicolas Flamel? The eldest of one of the worst families that has ever existed?"

The loyal members laughed once more.

Victor, Felix, and Perry exchanged solemn glances.

Felix apprehensively stepped forward and cried, "Surely, not *all* of us are bad, Your Highness?"

Minnie rolled her eyes. Even when he was being blatantly insulted, Felix was still fishing for compliments from Arthur. Incidentally, Arthur had none to give.

"All of you are rotten apples clinging to a dying tree," Arthur spat, "And one day, that tree is going to be consumed by fire."

"Ah, R," Nicolas grunted, "Hasn't Merlin taught you anything?"

Arthur angrily spun around.

Nicolas was still lying on the ground.

Yet, something was shining in his eyes.

"We may be consumed by the fire," Nicolas quietly said, "But you can *bet* that we'll rise from the ashes!"

Minnie blinked and suddenly Nicolas was on his feet. He gracefully twirled around to avoid Arthur's blows. Victor let out a deafening cheer. In his excitement, he ended up blindly grabbing Felix's shoulder. Felix didn't cheer, though his mouth turned up at the ends. Perry caught Minnie's eye and winked. Minnie beamed as she realized that Nicolas had been bluffing all along. He was now expertly wielding his blade, planning everything three moves in advance. His eyes were lit up with the typical Flamel fire. Arthur staggered backwards to avoid his blade. He wasn't quick enough and he ultimately ended up falling out of the ring.

Victor, Perry, and Minnie practically screamed.

Their pride for Nicolas was utterly overwhelming.

There was even something glinting in Felix's eyes. He quickly smothered it as he helped a very irate Arthur to his feet. The rest of the Brotherhood didn't dare to cheer, though their pride was evident. The only exceptions were Miss Kiss and Dmitri, who happily clapped.

A few of Arthur's loyal supporters grouped around him and whispered words of comfort.

"It doesn't matter," Arthur eventually boomed, "Because Nicolas can never be King."

He towered over Victor and added, "Are you so arrogant that you've forgotten your brother's sacrifice? Have you forgotten the deal which he bestowed to save your life?"

"No," Victor retorted, "I haven't forgotten."

"Then why have Nicolas duel me?"

"Because," Victor quietly said, "I wanted to make sure that everyone here knew that you would never have achieved the crown otherwise."

The Brotherhood was unable to hide their gasps and guffaws.

"Nicolas Flamel will always be the true King of the Brotherhood of Merlin," Victor passionately said, "And don't you dare forget it."

He walked away without another word, leaving an awkward silence in his wake.

Nicolas rubbed the back of his neck. He ultimately realized that he would benefit greatly from being anywhere else than right there. As such, he raced after his brother.

Minnie went to follow but Perry stopped her.

"I think that the two of them need to talk for a bit," Perry thoughtfully said, "It's been long overdue."

Minnie hesitated before ultimately nodding.

"Besides," Perry added, "I know that you have questions."

"I always have questions," Minnie wryly said.

Perry chuckled before jerking her head.

Minnie followed her through the castle.

They finally entered a large room. Minnie briefly wondered if they had accidently stumbled upon a carpet shop. Dozens of them were hanging on the walls. Minnie flushed as she realized that they were actually tapestries.

Perry began to browse for several minutes.

Minnie's eyes fell upon a tapestry of the Brotherhood. They were at some sort of celebration. She grinned as she spotted a young teenager with black hair. He was happily dancing at the edge of the crowd.

"I thought that Victor didn't like dancing?" Minnie amusedly said.

"He doesn't," Perry remarked.

Minnie was taken aback.

Perhaps it was Nicolas?

"No," Perry chuckled, "It's not my husband. You didn't really think that the white hair was natural, did you?"

Minnie's eyes widened as she realized that the boy in the tapestry had golden eyes.

Perry continued to browse before calling Minnie's name.

She wheeled over and followed the plump woman's gaze.

Minnie's hands flew to her mouth.

The tapestry depicted a scene in the chamber where they had originally been summoned several days ago. Victor was on his hands and knees. It was one of the few times that she had ever seen him without his ponytail. Instead, his long hair was hanging over his face. The weaver of the tapestry had taken great care to show the fear in his purple eyes.

Her attention turned to the two figures in front of Victor.

Nicolas was standing tall and proud as he faced Arthur. His sword was raised and was clashing with Arthur's blade. Minnie realized with a bit of fascination that Nicolas was the one holding Excalibur. She also realized that the crown was on Nicolas' perfectly kempt bun.

The other members of the Brotherhood were crowded around the scene. Minnie spotted a smiling Perry. She also spotted Felix, standing behind Arthur, staring at his brother with a look of utmost horror. He wasn't the only one. Most of the Brotherhood looked shocked. Even Miss Kiss seemed taken aback. Minnie wasn't quite sure what was going on in the scene. Yet she had a feeling that it was something huge. Sheer power seemed to emit from the tapestry.

"What happened?" Minnie whispered.

Perry sadly smiled and said, "The pacifist fought back."

Minnie was still confused.

Perry was kind enough to explain, "This took place a few days after Merlin's untimely death. The Brotherhood was pretty...upset with Victor."

Minnie could only imagine.

"The other night," Perry continued, "You asked my brother-in-law why he wasn't killed for his actions. He nearly was. Of course, Nicolas was strictly against it. At the time, he was the true King of the Brotherhood. He and Arthur had spent years competing for the crown and sword. Nicolas had won. His ruling should have been final. Unfortunately, upon realizing that Victor was the one who had unintentionally to Merlin's death, Arthur called a secret meeting. He unofficially motioned for a vote. The majority ruled. Victor would be beheaded for his crimes."

Minnie shivered.

"Nicolas didn't have a choice," Perry sadly said, "He gave in to the Brotherhood's demands. The morning of the execution came. It was tense. It was extremely tense. Victor was a complete wreck. He knelt before Arthur. Arthur raised his sword..."

Perry broke off.

It was a moment before she whispered, "We could all hear the sound of the two blades colliding. It echoed throughout the entire chamber. It took us a moment to realize what had happened. Nicolas had stepped in front of Victor and had prevented his execution. I can still remember the exact words that he said. Of course, we spoke a bit differently back then. But he essentially said: 'Did you really think that I was going to let you kill my brother?'"

Minnie shivered.

She finally murmured, "That's not really fighting back though, is it? I mean, what Nicolas did is amazing. But he just prevented Arthur from doing something. He didn't really fight..."

"There's more to the story," Perry remarked, "Nicolas turned and faced Victor. I still remember their exact expressions. It was as if time had slowed down. Victor looked just as shocked as the rest of us. And then my husband told him to run."

"Did he?"

Perry nodded and said, "He staggered to his feet and raced away. Nicolas turned back to Arthur and the two slowly lowered their swords. Arthur essentially told Nicolas that he *was* going to kill Victor and that Nicolas was too weak to stop him."

"What happened?" Minnie gasped.

"Do you remember what the highest level of magic is?" Perry asked.

"The Push," Minnie retorted, "Victor said that it was essentially pushing out a surrounding wall of pure energy."

"Precisely," Perry quipped, "There's only one member of the Brotherhood of Merlin that can successfully perform this magic."

Minnie swallowed before whispering, "Nicolas."

Perry nodded.

She pushed the large tapestry aside to reveal another one.

This one was a close-up of Nicolas. Minnie stared at it in wonder. Nicolas' chin was touching his chest.

His eyes were closed. From this alone, he could have been peacefully meditating. Yet his arms were spread out to the side. Minnie could see chamber behind him. The weaver of the tapestry had taken great care to show the cracking windows and crumbling walls.

"He brought the house down," Minnie softly said.

Perry laughed and cried, "Pretty much."

Minnie could only gape at the tapestry.

"The Brotherhood was stunned," Perry continued, "There were only a few of us who knew about the great power that Nicolas held. A few even ran in fear. He was very careful, of course. He ensured everyone's safety. He merely wanted to show Arthur that crossing him was a very bad idea. I think that Arthur figured it out sometime between being swept off of his feet and being thrown into the back wall."

Minnie laughed.

"I often wonder what would have happened if Nicolas hadn't stopped himself," Perry admitted, "Arthur would have probably caved. He would have spared Victor's life. Nicolas would have continued to rule over the Brotherhood. Yet my husband had no interest in ruling with fear and power. And so, he opened his mind to the possibilities and he made a sacrifice."

Minnie remembered the cryptic poem from the other day.

She put two-and-two together.

She still let Perry finish the story.

"Nicolas made a deal with Arthur," Perry quietly said, "Arthur would be the King of the Brotherhood of Merlin so long as Victor was alive. Arthur would wield Excalibur so long as Victor was a member of the Brotherhood."

Minnie thought back to the conversation that had occurred the other night.

"Give me one good reason why I shouldn't kill you," Arthur had demanded.

Minnie had shivered at the malice his tone.

A twisted smile had formed on Victor's face.

"Because," Victor had simply said, "You hate the thought of my brother succeeding more than you hate the thought of me failing."

Minnie knew that Perry was reading her mind.

She nodded and said, "Arthur hates Victor for what he did to Merlin. He hates him with a passion. However, he will never act upon his hate. For he will never give up the crown. He still tries to make our lives hell. He immediately exiled us from the castle, he treats Victor like his own personal punching bag whenever they're together, he constantly insults us..."

She solemnly broke off.

Silence surrounded them for a moment.

"Why don't you just kill Arthur?" Minnie finally asked.

Perry laughed and cried, "Don't think that it hasn't crossed our minds."

"I mean, it would solve everything," Minnie pointed out, "Nicolas could become the king, the three of you could move back in, and the world would have one less jerk in it."

Perry sadly smiled and said, "It's not that simple."

"It never is," Minnie sighed.

"Especially when your husband's a pacifist," Perry added.

Minnie nodded and thought about their conversation last night.

She then thought about something that Rainwater had said.

"Who do you think is worse?" Minnie asked, "Arthur or Felix?"

"Neither."

Minnie confusedly glanced at her.

"It's hard to say which one is the worst," Perry simply said, "They've both done some great and evil things in their own way."

"Great things?" Minnie repeated.

Perry nodded.

"You're joking, right?"

"No," Perry replied, "I'm not."

Minnie didn't even know what to say.

She ultimately turned and wheeled away.

Perry let out a loud sigh.

Minnie honestly couldn't care less.

Felix was an irredeemable jerk. He would always be an irredeemable jerk. Nothing that anyone else said would prevent him from being an irredeemable jerk.

"Up until three months ago, you thought that Victor was an irredeemable jerk."

Minnie spun around.

Perry had followed her out into the corridor.

Minnie flushed and stammered, "T...that's different!"

"No, it's not," Perry gently said, "I'm not going to pretend that Felix is a saint but he's not completely evil. Nobody is. Not even him. I once told you that everybody had the potential to do something great. I meant that. Not everybody acts on that potential but they have it and it's important for you to realize that."

Minnie regarded her for a moment before asking, "Why are you telling me this?"

"Because it's important for you to know," Perry explained, "Because you have a very serious flaw, Minerva Banks. Don't looked so shocked. Everyone has at least one flaw. That's the point that I'm trying to make."

Heat had risen to Minnie's cheeks.

Her tone was harsh as she asked, "What's my flaw?"

"You have a very black-and-white view of the world," Perry explained, "You grew up thinking that The Quartet was wholly good and that Victor was wholly evil. Once you learned that Victor had done some good things and that Felix had done some bad things, you automatically assumed that the roles were reversed. You assumed that Victor was wholly good and that The Quartet was wholly evil. But you're wrong."

Minnie was furiously blushing.

She truly hated the fact that Perry could read her mind.

"I know you do," Perry gently said, "And I wouldn't ordinarily be giving this soap-box speech. The only reason why I'm even saying anything is because this pure hatred is going to eat you alive. You need to understand that the world cannot be split into good and evil. People are going to do both great and terrible things."

"What about the prophecy?" Minnie shot back, "The prophecy which divides everyone into Protagonists, Antagonists, and Neutrals?"

"The prophecy's bullshit!" Perry impatiently said.

Minnie laughed at that.

"Nobody is purely good, purely bad, or purely neutral," Perry went on, "That's why we choose to ignore the prophecy. By God, if we followed every single prophecy that was made, we wouldn't have any free will. But I digress...I know that you hate Felix. I know that you hate Victor's treatment of Felix. I know that Felix has done some truly hateful things. Yet he's not some sort of one-dimensional villain who's evil for the sake of being evil."

Minnie tried to let this sink in.

She hesitated before asking, "Do you think that he should have been at that Christmas party?"

"Absolutely not," Perry immediately said, "That was really stupid of Victor."

Minnie laughed.

"But we shouldn't murder him either," Perry continued, "Or Arthur."

Minnie flushed and cried, "I was joking!"

"No, you weren't," Perry remarked, "The point is that you and Victor were both wrong last night. In fact, both of your opinions on Felix are wrong. He's not a saint whose actions can be excused through blood relation. He's not a demon who causes fire with every touch. He's a human, just like the rest of us. Well, most of us. The sooner both of you learn that, the better."

Her tone was pointed.

Minnie turned and saw that Victor and Nicolas were standing behind her. The former looked unimpressed. The latter looked slightly amused.

"Sorry, Perenelle," Victor spoke up, "If I had

known that you were going to make a long-winded speech, I would have brought along a soap-box."

"Oh, shut up," Perry laughed, "You make pretentious speeches all the time!"

Minnie nodded in agreement.

"As much as I was enjoying your speech, love," Nicolas gently said, "I'm afraid that I'm going to have to have to cut it short. The next challenge is about to begin."

"Oh yeah," Minnie muttered, "'Kinda forgot about those."

It had already been an incredibly long day.

She wheeled after the Flamels as they made their way to the dungeons. Arthur glared at them as they made their way through the crowd.

"Minerva," Arthur snapped, "You're first."

"What's the challenge?" Minnie warily asked.

Arthur didn't answer and instead held open a door.

Minnie took a deep breath before entering the chamber.

She didn't even flinch as the door slammed shut.

Minnie realized that this chamber didn't have a window.

She couldn't see the others.

She wondered if they could see her.

Minnie glanced ahead and found herself facing three different doors.

A gentle voice filled the room:
"How do you want to die?"

CHAPTER ELEVEN

Minnie's heart skipped a beat.

The gentle voice repeated its question:

"How do you want to die?"

"W...what?" Minnie stammered.

"How do you want—?"

"I heard you," Minnie snapped.

"How do you want to die?"

Minnie rolled her eyes and cried, "I don't."

"How do you want to die?"

"I don't want to die."

"Beg pardon, Minerva," Arthur's voice rang out, "Technical difficulties. One moment..."

Minnie impatiently waited.

"There we are," Arthur continued, "Have fun dying."

His voice was replaced by the gentle one:

"How do you want to die? The first door leads to a pit of spikes. The second door leads to a chamber of fire. The third door leads to a manticore that hasn't been fed in years. You must go through one of the doors. You may ask me five questions."

"What?" Minnie shrieked, "Why do I have to choose one of the doors?"

"Those count as two questions."

Minnie internally kicked herself.

The voice answered her rhetorical questions:

"You must choose as it is the only way to earn points for the challenge."

"Can I just go back out the door that I came in?"

"You cannot. You have two questions left."

Minnie took a deep breath and tried to think.

One door led to a pit of spikes.

The second door led to a chamber of fire.

The third door led to a manticore that hadn't eaten in months.

Minnie remembered the manticore from the zoo; it had looked terrifying! She was not about to face that. She also had no idea how she could get her wheelchair over a pit of spikes.

"Is there a fire extinguisher that I can use?" Minnie hopefully asked.

"There is not. You have one question left."

Minnie groaned and muttered, "Can't you just tell me which door to use?"

"I cannot. You have no questions left."

Minnie loudly swore.

"What happens if I ask another question?" Minnie hotly asked.

"You have no questions left."

"What's 2+2?"

"You have no questions left."

"What's the meaning of life?"

"You have no questions left."

"Are you just a voice or do you belong to a body?"

"You have no questions left."

"Alright, alright," Minnie snarled.

She apprehensively stared at each of the doors.

The gentle voice flooded the room:

"You must choose."

"I'm trying!"

Three doors.

The first led to a pit of spikes.

The second led to a chamber of fire.

The third led to a manticore that hadn't been fed in months.

A manticore that hadn't been fed in...

Minnie groaned.

She wheeled over to the third door and wrenched it open.

A horrible stench caused her to clamp a hand over her nose.

It was just as she suspected.

The manticore was dead.

It hadn't been fed in three months.

Minnie shook her head and briefly wondered if the other doors really had led to deadly consequences. She wasn't about to find out. She wheeled through the revolting room and entered another door. This one led to a spiraling corridor which ultimately led back to the main dungeons. Her friends immediately surrounded her, though their noses wrinkled.

Arthur sighed and growled, "Well done, Minerva.

Minnie thanked him and was forced out of the corridor. Minnie knew that it was to prevent her from telling the others the answer. She only hoped that Perry had read her mind.

She made her way back up to her room. She spent the rest of the day replying to angry emails from her professors. She finally fell asleep. The week was definitely catching up to her.

Victor shook her awake several hours later.

"Oh good," Minnie sleepily said, "You're alive."

"I wouldn't have died, anyway," Victor pointed out, "I'm immortal, remember?"

Minnie yawned and asked, "So, what was the point of the challenge?"

"To kill you," Victor simply said.

Minnie accepted this answer.

She realized that Victor had been kind enough to bring up a plate of food. Minnie dug in, used the bathroom, changed into her pajamas, and fell asleep once more.

She woke up several hours later and saw that moonlight was pouring through the window. Victor was snoring on the other side of the room. Minnie rolled over but couldn't get back to sleep. She eventually got up and started to wheel through the castle. She didn't have a particular destination in mind. She was just trying to clear her head.

She ultimately heard whispering and glanced into a chamber. She realized that the whispering was from Miss Kiss. She also realized that Miss Kiss was talking to herself.

Minnie couldn't hear what she was saying yet she could hear the gentleness in her voice.

Yet there was something eerie about the scene. Minnie felt the hairs on the back of her neck stand up. She wheeled forward and the door creaked.

Miss Kiss glanced up before smiling.

"Sorry," Minnie cried, "I was just—"

"No need to apologize," Miss Kiss gently said, "One moment, please."

She turned back to the empty room and said, "Shall we talk tomorrow night?"

Minnie gave a start before saying, "Sure?"

"Not you, dear," Miss Kiss called.

Minnie watched as she dipped into a low bow.

Minnie unintentionally shivered.

Miss Kiss straightened up and amusedly asked, "How confused are you right now?"

"A bit," Minnie admitted.

Miss Kiss laughed before saying, "I Mastered in Mediumship. I can see spirits."

Minnie's jaw dropped open.

At long last, she stammered, "Th...there was a ghost in here?"

"A spirit," Miss Kiss corrected, "And yes."

"Ghosts are real?"

"Spirits."

Minnie swallowed.

Miss Kiss tilted her head and asked, "Are you alright?"

"Sure," Minnie squeaked, "It's not the weirdest thing that I've heard this week."

Miss Kiss chuckled.

"Who was the spirit?" Minnie curiously asked.

Miss Kiss opened her mouth before promptly shutting it.

Minnie turned and felt her heart plummet.

The Quartet was standing behind her.

"Isn't it past your bedtime?" Felix taunted.

"What do you want?" Minnie warily asked.

"Nothing to do with you," Felix retorted, "I'm off to help King Arthur set up the challenges for tomorrow."

He had drawn himself up.

"I have some lip balm upstairs if you need it," Minnie offered.

Felix blinked.

"You know," Minnie continued, "Just in case your lips get sore from kissing his ass."

Felix rolled his eyes and Minnie smirked.

Miss Kiss cackled.

"I curse the day that you joined my blasted brother," Felix muttered.

"That was your fault," Minnie pointed out, "You shouldn't have had your lackeys send me to New Quartz General in the first place."

Felix raised an eyebrow before saying, "I admit that said plan was a mistake on my part."

"So why'd you do it?"

"Excuse me?"

"Why did you send me to the hospital?" Minnie demanded.

It was something that she had been wondering for a while.

"Was all of it just a sick game in order to mess with me?" Minnie wondered, "Why would you have me break into someone's office and steal evidence of embezzlement if you were just going to destroy it? You must've known that I would see what it was."

"Actually, no," Felix admitted, "I didn't know that."

Minnie stared at him for a moment before it hit her.

"You didn't think that I would make it to his office," Minnie whispered.

"You weren't supposed to even make it past the lobby," Felix snarled, "Nor would you have, if my brother hadn't showed up. We certainly didn't expect that nor did we expect the two of you to work together nor did we expect you to beautifully stab him in the back."

Minnie felt a pang of guilt.

It quickly faded away as something occurred to her.

"Wait a minute," Minnie slowly said, "How'd you know that I stabbed Victor in the back?"

Felix looked annoyed.

"W...were you there?" Minnie stammered.

"I don't have time to entertain the narrow-mindset of a retard," Felix snapped, "If you'll excuse me..."

He began to walk away.

"You still didn't answer my main question," Minnie called, "Why did you send me to the hospital in the first place?"

Felix turned with an odd sort of smile on his face.

It caused a shiver to run down Minnie's spine.

"Because," Felix simply said, "You were the perfect candidate."

"What?"

He walked away without another word.

Minnie hesitated before following him.

"Minnie," Miss Kiss called, "Minnie, wait!"

Felix quickened his pace until he was running.

Minnie followed him across the entrance hall and watched as he burst outside. Minnie did the same. Unfortunately, the moon only provided so much light. Minnie struggled to wheel across the hilly grounds. She looked around and was dismayed to see that Felix was long gone.

What did he mean?

She was the perfect candidate for what?

Minnie went to turn around but the grass snagged her wheels.

She cried out as she ultimately ended sliding down a steep slope. She fell from her wheelchair and landed in the mud. She was simply glad that Felix hadn't been there to witness it.

Minnie pulled herself back into her wheelchair and glanced around.

She was sitting next to a small lake.

"MINERVA!"

Minnie turned at the alarmed shout.

Victor was racing towards her. His face was as white as the face of the moon. He reached Minnie and immediately began to tug at her chair.

"Hey," Minnie cried, "What are you doing?"

"Come on," Victor breathlessly said, "We need to get out of here. We need to get out of here right now. Let's get out of here. Let's go. Come on!"

Minnie gave a start.

Victor's calm and reserved demeanor had been

replaced by a frantic and feverish one. It was as if he was a completely different person. For a moment, she wondered if he was really Felix in disguise. Yet his eyes were purple. They were also filled with fear.

He quickly pushed Minnie back to the castle.

They burst into the entrance hall and Victor promptly collapsed.

He crouched down and clutched the top of his head.

"Victor?" Minnie worriedly said.

A crowd quickly formed. The other members of the Brotherhood looked just as confused as Minnie felt. She realized that Arthur's lip was curling. Felix was donning a strange expression; a mixture of a smirk and a frown. It made him look constipated. Nicolas and Perry pushed through the crowd, the former demanding to know what had happened.

"I...I couldn't sleep," Minnie stammered, "I went out onto the grounds and ended up falling down the hill. I was next to a lake and—"

"That'll do it," Perry murmured.

Her statement was nearly lost to the gasps that rang throughout the hall.

"Alright, alright," Nicolas thundered, "Everyone carry on."

The crowd reluctantly dispersed.

Only Arthur and Felix remained.

Nicolas and Perry crouched down on either side

of Victor. They whispered words of comfort until he was able to pull himself together. Victor finally nodded and mumbled that he was alright. His brother and sister-in-law helped him to his feet.

Victor rubbed the back of his neck and mumbled, "'Sorry about that."

"Don't be," Minnie immediately said.

Victor glanced at Arthur and Felix.

Oddly enough, the two had nothing to say.

"Come on," Nicolas gently said, "I have a few elixirs in my bedroom."

Victor nodded and gratefully followed his brother.

Minnie watched them go before whispering, "Well, that was unexpected."

Perry laughed.

"I've never seen Victor like that," Minnie added, "Have you?"

"Yes," Perry admitted, "On rare occasions."

She looked slightly troubled.

Minnie hesitated before asking, "Why is Victor afraid of the lake?"

"He's not afraid of the lake," Perry quietly said, "He's afraid of what's in it."

CHAPTER TWELVE

People were staring at Victor - and they weren't being subtle about it.

His cheeks reddened and he poked at his eggs.

"Who cares what they think?" Dmitri bracingly said.

"I do," Victor remarked.

"Well, you shouldn't."

"Well, I do."

Nicolas put a hand on his brother's shoulder.

"Stare back," Minnie whispered.

"Sorry?"

"Stare back," Minnie repeated, "Trust me."

Victor glanced at the group of onlookers. Their cheeks reddened and they finally looked away. A smile spread across Victor's face.

"Works like a charm," Minnie cheerfully said, "I'm sorry, again, about last night."

"Don't be," Victor remarked.

Minnie's remark was drowned out by Arthur's booming announcement:

"THE NEXT CHALLENGE IS ABOUT TO BEGIN!"

"Hooray," Minnie muttered.

Nicolas chuckled and said, "Let's head for the dungeons."

"Ah, ah," Arthur called, "We won't be going to

the dungeons for this one."

The group exchanged confused glances.

"Follow me," Arthur ordered.

The Brotherhood complied.

Minnie had to wait to use the elevator. She and Victor finally emerged in the entrance hall. Arthur impatiently ushered them along. Minnie was distinctly reminded of when she was in grade school and was shepherded by the stern teachers.

The Brotherhood followed Arthur outside. Victor helped Minnie across the rolling hills of the grounds. Minnie gasped as she recognized their destination. She could feel Victor stiffen.

"No," Nicolas spoke up, "No!"

"You can't do this" Perry burst out.

Dmitri ducked behind Miss Kiss.

Arthur merely smirked.

Felix came up next to him and mirrored the expression.

The group was next to the small lake. Several beams were hovering over the water. A glowing crystal was floating in the center.

"The object of the challenge is simple," Arthur cried, "You must simply retrieve the crystal. You cannot fly. You cannot touch the water. May Merlin's Spirit help you if you do."

Victor had begun to shake.

Minnie reached over and squeezed his arm.

The golden light appeared.

Victor took several deep breaths but it did little to calm him.

"You're making a huge mistake," Nicolas growled, "Stop this!"

Arthur ignored him.

Nicolas' outburst encouraged a few other members to protest. Their protests fell upon deafened ears as Arthur ordered Dmitri to go first. The Brotherhood anxiously watched as the child made his way across the beams. At one point, he teetered and cried out. Perry gasped. Nicolas pulled her into a tight hug. Victor ultimately wrenched away from Minnie and raced away.

Minnie was left wringing her hands.

She wasn't sure what was in the lake.

Yet the Brotherhood was clearly afraid.

That was enough to frighten her.

Dmitri teetered again and screamed for help.

"Stop screaming, kid," Victor called, "You're going to wake her."

The Brotherhood craned their necks. A breeze rustled their hair and clothes. Minnie's mouth fell open as she realized that Victor was riding Firestone. He steered the griffin close to the lake. Dmitri grabbed onto its mane and allowed himself to be carried away. Victor flew towards the crystal. Dmitri clung onto the mane with one hand and grabbed the crystal with the other. Victor safely flew the three of them back to the shore. Dmitri dropped down and handed the crystal to an exasperated Arthur. The King of the Brotherhood ultimately casted a spell that sent the crystal back to the center of the lake. Victor cheerfully called out for the next person.

He spent the rest of the day ushering people across the lake. He took care to help Minnie onto the griffin's back, just as he had done the other night. Several members of the Brotherhood giggled until Victor sharply told them all to shut up. Victor even flew Felix there and back.

Only Nicolas refused a ride.

Instead, the forty-year-old calmly walked around the perimeter of the lake until he was standing on the opposite side. Minnie watched as he took a deep breath and closed his eyes.

The wind picked up.

A crackle was in the air.

The Brotherhood slowly looked around before glancing at one another.

A smile spread across Victor's face.

A frown spread across Arthur's.

Perry looked madly in love.

Nicolas spread out his arms. Minnie threw on her brakes as a strange sort of wind hit the Brotherhood. The wall of energy crashed into the crystal and sent it flying.

Victor calmly caught it.

Nicolas walked back over and took the crystal from his brother.

"Well, then," Nicolas calmly said, "Since everyone has retrieved the crystal, I believe that everyone receives one-hundred points."

"Not everyone," Dmitri cried, "Arthur still hasn't gone."

"Quite right," Victor agreed, "Do be careful, Arthur. Don't touch the water."

The Brotherhood contained their snickers as they walked away.

Victor flew Firestone back to the zoo before joining the others in the dining hall.

"So," Minnie cheerfully said, "Have you conquered your fear?"

"Absolutely not," Victor retorted.

In fact, he looked rather ill.

He finally retreated to the bedroom.

Minnie spent the rest of the day hanging out with Nicolas, Perry, Dmitri, and Miss Kiss.

By the time the sun dipped beneath the horizon, they had all grown increasingly worried about Victor. They finally went up to the bedroom. Victor was lying in his bed. He was as pale as the sheets. Minnie could tell that he had recently vomited.

"That's it," Nicolas firmly said, "We're taking you to see Gwen."

"Gwen?" Minnie repeated.

"She Mastered in Healing," Nicolas explained, "Come on, Victor."

"No," Victor grunted, "I'm fine."

He went to stand up and promptly collapsed.

He grabbed the handle of Minnie's wheelchair for support.

"You're not fine," Miss Kiss insisted, "Let Gwen look at you."

Victor shook his head and muttered, "I've heard about how she heals the other members of the Brotherhood. I don't want that kind of healing."

He paused before adding, "Or do I?'

Perry amusedly hit him.

Minnie, Miss Kiss, and Nicolas did the same.

Even Dmitri slapped him.

"Hang on," Victor exclaimed, "Do you even know why you're hitting me?"

"No," Dmitri innocently said, "I just thought that it would be fun."

Minnie followed the four to the west wing of the castle. They finally stopped outside a golden door. Nicolas bravely knocked and it swung open.

Minnie caught a glimpse of a beautiful bedroom before Gwen blocked her view.

"What do you want?" Gwen coldly asked.

"Victor's ill," Nicolas declared.

"Pardon me if I don't give a damn."

Gwen went to slam the door.

Minnie caught it.

"Help him," Minnie ordered, "Or I'll tell Arthur about Lancelot."

Gwen's eyes widened and she hissed, "You wouldn't."

"Try me," Minnie retorted.

The women stared each other down for several minutes. Neither one refused to back down. They hardly even blinked. Minnie realized that Gwen's eyes were the same shade of red as her husband's. She briefly wondered what color Lancelot's eyes were. She turned her thoughts back to the situation at hand. She kept her face hardened as she metaphorically stood her ground.

"Damn," Miss Kiss finally whispered.

Even Minnie was surprised by her bravado.

Her shock escalated as Gwen finally muttered that she would heal him. They followed the irate woman to a small chamber. Minnie shivered as she realized that it was a hospital room.

Perry and Miss Kiss both slipped off their shoes.

This wasn't unnoticed by Minnie.

A small smile formed on her face. It faded away as Victor hopped up onto the table.

Gwen did a brief examination before saying, "You're experiencing physical side-effects from extreme anxiety; no doubt stimulated by today's challenge."

Her heels clicked as she walked around the hospital room.

Minnie uncomfortably grimaced.

"Are you alright?" Victor abruptly asked.

Minnie gave a start and cried, "Don't worry about me."

"I'm always worried about you," Victor teased.

Dmitri let out a soft giggle.

Minnie honestly wasn't sure what to say.

"There's not much that I can do to help you," Gwen declared, "Even the most advanced magic can't cure anxiety. Any elixirs that your brother and sister-in-law make will result in nasty side-effects. I'd say that the best bet is for you to withdrawal from this competition."

She was giving him a vile smirk.

"Thanks for the advice," Victor remarked, "It's a good thing that I never follow my doctor's orders."

"I'm not your doctor."

"All the more reason to not listen to you," Victor remarked, "Come on."

He hopped down and left.

The group, minus Gwen, headed back to the guest chambers. Minnie tried to hide a smile as she realized that Miss Kiss and Perry were carrying their shoes. The women, Nicolas, and Dmitri fussed over Victor for another hour or so. His eyes finally closed.

Nicolas, Perry, Dmitri, and Miss Kiss bade Minnie goodnight before tiptoeing away.

Minnie used the bathroom, changed into her pajamas, and hopped into her own bed.

Minnie found herself staring at the ceiling.

She was sure that Victor had gone to sleep.

She subsequently jumped as his voice floated across the room:

"What are you thinking about?"

Minnie took a deep breath and said, "Never trust someone who wears high heels in a hospital."

"What?" Victor snorted.

"Never trust someone who wears high heels in a hospital," Minnie repeated, "It's something that I used to say when I was younger."

"And why, pray tell, would Young Minerva Banks say that?" Victor amusedly asked.

"Young Minerva Banks would say that because Young Minerva Banks watched way too many medical shows," Minnie explained, "I always hated it whenever they showed the patients wearing high heels. And so I would always say, 'Never trust someone who wears high heels in a hospital.'"

"But why?"

Minnie chose her words carefully as she said, "That's not how it works in hospitals. A hospital is one of the last places in the world where you should dress to impress. First of all, when you're in a hospital, do you know how exhausting and painful it is to even get out of bed to use the bathroom, let alone make yourself look presentable?"

"Yeah," Victor agreed, "It's tough."

"Secondly," Minnie continued, "Do you realize how much foul liquids you're going to be stepping in at a hospital? You don't want to wear an expensive pair of heels. You want something on your feet that's comfortable and that's not going to be missed if soiled."

She took a deep breath and went on, "Finally, and most importantly, people don't care. They don't care what you look like. They don't care what outfit you're wearing. They don't care what's on your feet. The only thing that they care about is your health. So there's no need to impress anyone."

She could hear low chuckling from the other side of the room.

"What?" Minnie defensively said.

"Nothing," Victor gently said, "Nothing at all."

Silence filled the room for a few moments.

It was broken as Victor whispered, "Never trust someone who wears high heels in a hospital."

Minnie smiled and said, "Never trust someone who wears high heels in a hospital."

CHAPTER THIRTEEN

Victor looked considerably better the next morning.

He and Minnie continued to talk about hospital fashion as they made their way to the dining hall. They joined Nicolas, Perry, Miss Kiss, and Dmitri. Minnie had just enough time to dig into her pancakes when Arthur cried, "Our next challenge—"

"Yeah, yeah," Minnie interjected, "Jeez, you're like a broken record."

Snorts and giggles swept through the dining hall.

Arthur glared at her before saying, "Be down in the dungeons in five minutes."

He stomped away without another word.

"You're really getting to him," Miss Kiss proudly said.

Minnie grinned as they entered the corridor.

She waited for the elevator and slipped inside as soon as the doors opened. Someone pushed past her and quickly hit the button to close the doors. Victor cried out. Minnie's hand found her scabbard as Felix threw her a vile smirk.

Things didn't improve as the elevator abruptly screeched to a halt.

"My my," Felix softly said.

Minnie groaned.

She impatiently waited but the elevator remained in place.

She hit the wall.

It refused to budge.

She smacked it again, for good measure.

Nothing.

"A brilliant strategy," Felix taunted, "I can't imagine why it didn't work."

"Shut up," Minnie muttered.

Felix continued to make snide remarks.

Minnie was able to tune most of them out.

She only looked up when Felix said, "I have no idea why my brother likes you."

"Funny," Minnie coolly said, "I was going to say the same about you."

"My relationship with Victor isn't ideal," Felix admitted, "Nor do I want it to be. However, at least our relationship isn't built on pity."

"What are you talking about?"

"Well, that's not true," Felix continued, "I do sort of pity him. Yet it's not the main staple of our relationship."

"Good to know," Minnie remarked.

She began inspecting the buttons.

"Is your intelligence so low that you cannot even understand what I'm saying?"

"I understand what you're getting at," Minnie cried, "I just have bigger problems at the moment."

"Haven't you ever wondered why my brother hired you?" Felix quietly asked.

Minnie swallowed before murmuring, "Not once."

She was lying.

Felix knew it.

"He pitied you," Felix snarled, "That's the only reason that he took you in and that's the only reason that he hasn't kicked you to the curb. You really think that a sixteen-hundred-year-old sorcerer wants to hang out with a poor, black, retard?"

Minnie's throat was raw.

Nevertheless, she kept her voice even as she asked, "Is there any point to this rant or do you just like hearing yourself speak?"

"The point is," Felix hissed, "You're wasting your time. You're never really going to be a member of the Brotherhood of Merlin. The fact that you even think that you have a chance makes me question your intelligence even more."

"Victor thinks that I can do it," Minnie firmly said, "So do Nicolas and Perry."

"Oh grow up, Minerva," Felix spat, "How many times have people told you that you could do something because they didn't want to make the little retard feel bad?"

Minnie was taking deep breaths.

The lights in the elevator were blinding.

Fortunately, Felix's next sentence was drowned out by a loud whirring noise.

Minnie sighed with relief as the elevator descended.

She wheeled out as soon as the doors were open.

A crowd was on the other side.

Victor practically threw people aside.

"Minerva," Victor cried, "Are you alright?"

"Yeah," Minnie hoarsely said.

He put a hand on her shoulder and asked, "What did he do?"

"N...nothing."

"Minerva..."

"He said some stuff," Minnie muttered, "That's it."

"What did he say?"

"It's not important."

"Of course it is," Victor immediately said, "It obviously has you rattled."

Minnie sighed.

All at once, she blurted out, "Why did you hire me?"

"What?"

"Why did you hire me?"

Victor's cheeks reddened.

He checked his watch and muttered, "Come on; we need to get to the next challenge."

He spun around and walked away without another word.

Minnie reluctantly glanced over her shoulder.

Felix was smirking.

Minnie's mind buzzed. She was unable to focus. She kept thinking about what Felix had said. Perry tried to pull her aside twice but Minnie refused to listen to anything that she had to say. Minnie knew that it was irrational. She knew that Felix was lying.

Then again...

Minnie could barely concentrate through the challenge.

She would have probably failed anyway.

Arthur merely went around and asked people trivial questions about magic, Merlin, and the history of the Brotherhood. Minnie had no idea what the answers were. This didn't help boost her confidence at all. Each passing minute brought another knot to her stomach.

She was aware of the fact that Victor, Nicolas, and Perry were worriedly whispering.

They were worried about her.

They didn't think that she could do it.

Minnie's throat closed.

She turned and quickly wheeled away.

She didn't have a destination in mind.

Or did she?

Minnie ensured that nobody was looking before

slipping through a door. She followed the long tunnel down to the unicorn's grove. Rainwater gently greeted her. Minnie tapped her scabbard and threw it onto the ground. She sat down in the grass and Rainwater knelt next to her. After receiving permission, Minnie stroked the unicorn's long hair.

The simple act helped her feel better.

Rainwater told her stories of the brave soldiers of olde who fought for justice and liberty.

The stories gave her the strength that she so desperately needed.

She only looked up when it began to steadily rain.

Minnie was shocked when she realized that the moon was up.

She also realized that she really needed to use the bathroom!

And so, she thanked the unicorns and retrieved her sword. She made the long journey back through the corridor. She was startled to see that the dungeons were empty.

Minnie flushed as she realized that she had been in the grove for hours.

She checked her phone and realized that she had several missed texts from Victor. They stated that the Brotherhood was having a meeting in the chamber where they had first arrived.

Minnie rode the elevator up to the floor.

She got lost twice but was eventually able to retrace her wheels back to the right corridor.

The chamber door was ajar.

Minnie could hear Victor's voice.

"Leave her alone, R," Victor was saying, "She's not a threat to you. She's not a threat to the Brotherhood. She's not a threat to anyone. She's a poor black woman in a wheelchair. If you're intimidated by *that* then—"

"Victor, shut up!" Perry abruptly hissed.

Minnie had no doubt that Perry could hear her thoughts. Said thoughts were comprised of multiple curses and some rather vile nicknames for Victor. Minnie felt as though she had been slapped. No. A slap would have hurt less. Every bit of confidence that the unicorns had given her had crumbled away. She wheeled forward so that she was in the doorway.

Victor immediately rose and whispered her name.

"Sorry," Minnie cheekily said, "I didn't mean to interrupt. I'll just be on my way and you guys can get back to talking about me."

She turned and wheeled away.

She wasn't quite sure how she had managed to make it back to their room. She had been blinded by stinging tears. She could hear Victor running after her.

Minnie reached the room first. She slammed the door and locked it.

The doorknob jiggled and Victor frantically called her name.

Minnie rolled her wet eyes and cried, "Can I help you?"

"Let me in!"

"No!"

"Minerva, please!"

"Nope!"

Minnie's tone was light though she was internally crumbling. Victor had brought up her race, gender, ability, and socioeconomic status before. However, there had always been the implication that no matter what the rest of the world thought, he didn't really care about any of it.

Tonight had been the first time where Victor had blatantly insulted her. He hadn't known that she was listening but that made it even worse.

How many other times had he said those things?

There was a gentler knock on the door.

"Minnie?" Perry called, "Are you okay?"

"No," Minnie admitted.

"Can we come in?" Nicolas asked.

When Minnie hesitated, Perry added, "Victor isn't with us."

Minnie sighed and unlocked the door.

Nicolas and Perry walked in.

"Listen," Perry immediately said, "I know that you're upset but Victor—"

"—is currently hanging off of the balcony," Nicolas abruptly said.

Minnie's jaw dropped as she realized that Nicolas was right.

Victor had apparently scaled the side of the castle and was now clinging onto the balcony railing. He was trying to pull himself up. He was also failing to do so.

Minnie, Perry, and Nicolas raced onto the balcony.

"What the hell are you doing?" Perry exclaimed.

"I needed to talk to Minerva," Victor wheezed.

"Are you crazy?" Minnie shrieked, "You're going to end up slipping and falling!"

"No, I won't."

Victor ended up slipping and falling.

Minnie watched in horror as he lost his grip and ended up toppling backwards. Her scream drowned out his own as he plummeted to the ground. She flinched at the squelching noise that occurred when his body hit the wet grass. She realized that Nicolas and Perry weren't that perturbed. They had spent sixteen-hundred years watching Victor fall from various places.

Nevertheless, they joined Minnie in peering over the railing.

Victor was lying motionless on the ground.

Minnie spun around and hurried through the

castle. Nicolas and Perry quickly followed suit. The three burst through the main doors and hurried through the drenched grounds. They finally reached Victor. Minnie fell from her chair and knelt next to him in the sopping grass.

"I'm fine," Victor grunted, "I'm alright."

"You idiot," Minnie cried, "Why the hell would you climb a balcony in the rain?"

Victor slowly sat up and said, "I needed to talk to you and you had locked the door."

"You can fly," Minnie exclaimed, "And you have a pet griffin!"

"Firestone isn't my pet," Victor remarked.

The rain was soaking everyone's clothes to their skin.

Minnie shivered.

Victor reached for her shoulder but she shied away.

"Minerva," Victor pressed, "Let me talk..."

"Alright," Minnie sighed, "Talk."

"I didn't mean to insult you," Victor quietly said, "I was trying to get Arthur to underestimate you. In case you haven't noticed, that's one of our greatest strategies. If he thinks that you pose no threat, you'll have the upper hand if a future fight occurs."

Minnie let this sink in.

At long last, she whispered, "You didn't mean...?"

"Of course not," Victor retorted, "You know me better than that."

"Do I?" Minnie shot back.

Victor looked startled.

"I barely know anything about you," Minnie exclaimed, "The things that I *do* know, I've either had to piece together or have had other people tell me. You've been lying and keeping me in the dark about things from the moment that I met you!"

Victor looked slightly offended as he said, "When have I ever done that?"

"Are you serious?" Minnie cried, "You didn't even tell me that Felix was a corrupt jerk. You waited until *after* I gave him the envelope. Why the hell did you do that? Do you know how much time and frustration we could have saved if you had been like, 'By the way, Minerva, I am really on your side whereas Felix is going to double-cross you'? It would have made things so much easier in the long run! But, no, you remained all mysterious and subsequently caused a huge series of events that could have all been avoided if you had just been upfront and honest!"

"Would you have believed me?" Victor asked.

Minnie hesitated before admitting that he had a point.

At long last, she muttered, "Fair point."

"No, you're right," Victor gently said, "From this moment on, I'll be upfront and honest."

Minnie was skeptical.

"I promise," Victor insisted.

"Fine," Minnie cynically said, "What happened to Merlin?"

"I don't remember."

Minnie amusedly rolled her eyes as Nicolas and Perry chuckled.

"Come on," Perry gently spoke up, "We're all going to get pneumonia if we're out here for much longer."

Victor helped Minnie back into her wheelchair.

The four hurried inside and dried off.

Questions still tugged at the back of Minnie's mind.

Her stomach churned as they became louder and louder.

She wasn't able to get any sleep.

She kept seeing Felix's smirk every time that she closed her eyes.

CHAPTER FOURTEEN

Minnie poured herself a third cup of coffee.

Perry chuckled and muttered, "You really are a graduate student."

"What gave it away?" Minnie wryly asked, "The twitching eye or the bag beneath it?"

"Both."

"Can you pass the ketchup?" Victor spoke up.

Minnie practically threw it at him. Eyebrows went up but not a word was spoken. Heat rose to Minnie's cheeks. She supposed that she still wasn't over the argument last night.

Arthur rose to his feet and gained everyone's attention.

Nearly the entire Brotherhood chorused, "The next challenge is about to begin."

Arthur frowned before sinking back into his seat.

"Is it me," Dmitri cried, "Or is he looking angrier and angrier?"

"We're all looking angrier and angrier," Perry solemnly said, "These challenges are getting to us; some more than others."

Minnie was thoroughly blushing.

The group made their way down to the dungeons for the umpteenth time. Arthur ushered everyone into one large chamber. He then held up a single medicine ball.

"This challenge is an interesting one," Arthur declared, "You will toss the ball to a person of your choosing. You will then ask them a question. They *must* answer truthfully."

"Are you kidding me?" Minnie blurted out, "One of your challenges is truth-or-dare?"

Several people laughed.

"There are no dares," Arthur replied, "Only truths."

Everyone sat down on the floor and began to throw the medicine ball around. One woman asked her husband if he had been having an affair. He had no choice but to affirm her suspicions. The secrets only escalated from there. The medicine ball finally reached Nicolas. A portly man asked him about his opinion of Arthur.

"I think that Arthur has been corrupted by hatred and greed," Nicolas replied.

He gently handed the medicine ball to his wife.

"Do you still love me, dear?" Nicolas asked.

Perry smiled and truthfully said, "Until the end of time."

The two shared a gentle kiss.

Perry handed the ball to Minnie and asked, "How are you holding up?"

Minnie glared at her before saying, "As well as the next guy."

Speaking of…

Minnie absentmindedly threw the ball towards Victor.

Nicolas and Perry straightened up.

Miss Kiss lifted her chin.

It took Minnie a moment to realize that she had been given a golden opportunity. She could ask Victor anything and he would have to truthfully answer. His purple eyes were sparkling with fear and dread.

Minnie went to ask the first question on her mind:

"What happened to Mer—?"

She paused.

Another question had occurred to her; one that was more important.

"Why did you hire me?"

Victor gave a start and cried, "What?"

"Why did you hire me?" Minnie repeated.

Victor took a deep breath before muttering, "I forfeit my points."

Minnie groaned.

"You can't," Arthur replied, "Answer the question."

Victor looked immensely uncomfortable.

At long last, he muttered, "Can I ask my question first?"

"I suppose."

Victor abruptly threw the ball. It crashed into

Felix's stomach. Felix had been kneeling and was subsequently knocked onto his back.

"What did you tell Minerva yesterday?" Victor demanded.

Felix reluctantly recounted what was said in the elevator.

"That's what I thought," Victor sighed, "Fine, Minerva, I'll answer your question. However, I refuse to do so in front of the kangaroo court. Let's go."

He stood up and Minnie pulled herself into her chair.

Nicolas, Perry, Dmitri, and Miss Kiss stood up as well.

"No," Victor immediately said.

They looked disappointed but ultimately sat back down.

Minnie followed Victor out into the corridor.

"If I'm going to confess this," Victor declared, "I'm going to be comfortable."

Several minutes later, Minnie was clinging onto a mixture of fur and feathers. Firestone was soaring high above the clouds.

Victor sat down next to her and said, "I can assure you that my reason for hiring you had nothing to do with pity."

Minnie wanted to believe him.

Yet she still had her doubts.

"Do you want to know the funny part?" Victor

thoughtfully asked, "Your actions last night are the perfect example of the main reason that I hired you."

Minnie uncomfortably squirmed as she remembered the events of last night.

"You were hurt," Victor continued, "You were angry. And yet, when I acted like an idiot and ultimately paid the price, you immediately made sure that I was alright."

He grinned at her and said, "I knew that I was going to hire you the minute that you sprayed The Quartet with hot coffee and hot tea. You still didn't trust me but you knew that I was in trouble. I've made a lot of mistakes in the past sixteen-hundred-years and I've lost a lot of good people. You've seen how Arthur treats me. You've seen how most of the Brotherhood treats me. It's very rare that someone actually sticks by me. You did. And I knew that I couldn't let that opportunity slip away. So I hired you in the hopes that you would continue to be by my side through thick or thin."

His tone was pure and genuine.

"Secondly," Victor continued, "I hired you because of your strength. I know, I know, you don't think that you're strong. You're wrong. You're one of the strongest, bravest, enduring—"

Minnie gave a start and asked, "Enduring?"

"You were in that pain chamber the longest," Victor pointed out, "Myself notwithstanding. I knew from the moment that I met you that you had endured a lot of pain and would continue to endure even more. I once told you that your will to fight outweighed our enemies' greatest strengths. I wasn't just being sappy. Well, I was, but I had a point. You're a fighter, Minerva Banks. I don't care what Nicolas says; I personally think that that's a great quality. I hope that you keep on fighting in the future."

Minnie beamed and whispered, "Don't worry; I will."

Her self-confidence was soaring as high as Firestone.

Her great mood lasted through the day.

She found herself smiling along with the other members of the Brotherhood as they watched Miss Kiss perform several songs. The Brotherhood was crowded in the beautiful ballroom, though they were merely spectators as Miss Kiss played the piano and sang. A band was backing her up. It was a much needed stress relief for everyone. The only ones missing were Arthur and Victor. The former refused to have fun and the latter was using the bathroom.

Minnie was sitting next to Perry, Nicolas, and Dmitri.

Miss Kiss finished a song and earned a round of ecstatic applause.

"Do you really want to know what happened to Merlin?" Perry abruptly asked.

Minnie blinked and cried, "What?"

"I know that it's what you really wanted to ask Victor," Perry explained, "Though, believe me, I'm glad that you asked him what you did. You needed to hear it and he needed to say it. But if you really want to know…"

"Perenelle," Nicolas spoke up, "Victor forbade us from telling her."

Perry abruptly smirked and said, "He said nothing about singing."

She gained Miss Kiss' attention and called, "Do you remember that little song that you wrote back in the 1920s?"

Miss Kiss grinned and said, "You know, Perry, I think I might."

She went over to the band and talked to them for a few moments. They eventually played a haunting jazz medley. A chill ran down Minnie's spine.

Miss Kiss hopped right up onto the piano.

She sat on the edge and began to sing:

Mamela, mamela, mamela

She held out the last note until she had everyone's attention. Only then did she continue:

Gather 'round, darlings
Listen to my hymn

If you ever fall in love
You'd better learn how to swim

The members of the Brotherhood all crowded around the piano. Most of them knew what the story was, yet they couldn't pass up listening to her outstanding voice. Miss Kiss continued:

Well, this here's the story
'Bout a humble gent
So young, so naïve
So innocent

Oh, he fell in love
With the Lady of the Lake
A sultry being
Named Nimue

Chini! Chini! Chini!
Into the water!
Chini! Chini! Chini!
Into the water!

Minnie swallowed.
So *that* was who Nimue was.
Perry squeezed her arm as Miss Kiss continued to sing:

He gave her his heart
And she stole his soul
That poor young gent
Was under her control

Every bit of lust
Fed into her power
And then one night
At the witching hour

The last note was practically shrieked.
Everyone shivered.
Minnie noticed that Perry had tears in her eyes.
Miss Kiss sang even slower:

She stepped out of the water
And walked on the land
She entered the castle
'Took a sorcerer's hand

She led him to the lake
Where he took his last breath
And that, my children, is the story
Of Merlin's death

Chini! Chini! Chini!
Into the water
Chini! Chini! Chini!

Into the water

That poor, young, gent
Knew that he was to blame
He spent centuries
Hanging his head in shame

So, my darlings
Don't be like him
If you ever fall in love
You'd better learn how to swim

If you ever fall in love
You'd better learn how to swim

The last lyric ended and was met with a chorus of applause.

Minnie's head was spinning.

"Victor's coming," Dmitri warned.

"Act natural," Perry hissed.

Victor entered the room.

He paused for a split second before muttering, "You told her."

Nobody met his gaze.

"Technically," Minnie sighed, "It was sung."

Victor groaned and everyone awkwardly apologized.

"So," Victor mumbled, "What do you think?"

Minnie took a deep breath before saying, "Never fall in love with a mysterious woman who emerges from the lake one day and gives your friend a sword."

Victor dryly chuckled. He wasn't as angry as Minnie had expected. On the contrary, he looked sad and exhausted.

"Look," Victor eventually said, "I understand if you want to leave after this."

Minnie snorted and asked, "Are you trying to get rid of me?"

Victor's eyes widened as he whispered, "Don't you want to leave?"

"No," Minnie remarked, "Why would I?"

Victor didn't answer.

Minnie was quickly able to put two-and-two together.

"Is *that* why you refused to tell me?" Minnie whispered, "You thought that I was going to leave when I found out the truth?"

Victor glumly nodded.

Minnie nudged him and said, "Hey, you're not getting rid of me that easily."

She sobered when she realized how small of a smile he had cracked.

"Victor," Minnie gently said, "I forgive you."

"You...you do?"

Minnie shrugged and nodded. Victor's face broke out into a true smile. For the first time in quite a long time, he actually looked hopeful.

"You're probably the only one that does," Victor finally admitted.

Perry swatted him and cried, "Don't be ridiculous; Nicolas and I forgive you!"

"We were technically never even angry at you," Nicolas pointed out.

Dmitri stepped forward and softly said, "I forgive you, Victor."

"As do I," Miss Kiss agreed, "I told you that you have friends here."

A thought occurred to her. Minnie watched with a bit of fascination as Miss Kiss stood right on the piano; in three-inch heels no less.

"Alright," Miss Kiss loudly said, "Let's put this to a vote – who forgives Victor?"

A few hands raised.

Victor wasn't that impressed.

"Keep in mind," Miss Kiss added, "That Arthur is not in the room nor do any of us have any intention of ratting you out."

Victor's jaw dropped as most of the Brotherhood raised their hands.

"You see," Miss Kiss gently said, "You're not as alone as you think."

Victor nodded.

His purple eyes were glistening.

Nicolas came to his rescue.

"Alright, alright," Nicolas called, "We only have a few hours until Arthur interrupts our breakfast with his annoying announcement."

Everyone laughed.

They all bade one another goodnight before retreating back to their rooms.

Minnie had just enough strength to use the bathroom, change into her pajamas, and fall into her bed. She was about to fall asleep when Victor called her name.

"Yeah?" Minnie sleepily asked.

"Thanks for standing by me."

Minnie grinned into her pillow before saying, "I don't stand by you."

"What are you...?"

"I don't stand by anyone."

She chuckled as Victor's pillow flew across the room.

CHAPTER FIFTEEN

"You are my one true love," Minnie whispered, "My one source of light in this world of never-ending darkness."

She brought the mug of coffee to her lips.

Victor, Nicolas, Perry, Miss Kiss, and Dmitri stared at her.

"What?" Minnie defensively said.

"You were doing so well yesterday," Perry remarked, "And now I'm questioning your sanity once again."

"We should always be questioning Minerva's sanity," Victor teased.

Minnie laughed alongside the others.

The laughter died down as Arthur stood up and cleared his throat.

"Three guesses what this is going to be about," Victor muttered.

Arthur made the announcement and the group went down to the dungeons.

"This is the most important challenge of the examination," Arthur softly said, "You will not be returning to this corridor afterword. You will instead exit into another room. You cannot perform any magic for this challenge. Doing so will disqualify you. I will enter this challenge first. A new person will enter every five minutes. Good luck."

Everyone exchanged glances as he slipped through the door.

Five minutes passed and Nicolas bravely entered.

Minnie and Victor exchanged nervous glances.

She began to wring her hands and he took them. The golden light wrapped around them.

He eventually stepped forward and entered the room.

Minnie warily watched as the population dwindled away. Her eyes widened as she realized that she and Felix were the only ones remaining in the corridor.

He gestured to the door and cried, "Ladies first."

Minnie rolled her eyes before entering.

She wheeled forward and threw on her brakes.

She was sitting on the edge of a cliff. A single staircase led to the ground below. Minnie squinted and could just make out an 'Exit' sign on the other side of the chasm.

But how to get to it?

There was nothing more than a ledge on the other side of the room.

Minnie supposed that the others could easily fly over.

She was not afforded with the same opportunity.

She began to grow frustrated.

There was no way that she was going to be able to get to the other side. She would simply have to forfeit the points. Minnie turned and tried to go back into the corridor.

The door was locked.

She nervously swallowed.

Jiggling the doorknob did nothing.

Banging on it was equally useless.

There was no way that she could go back.

She could only move forward.

Yet that seemed equally impossible.

Frustration and fear caused Minnie's heart to quicken its pace.

She honestly had no idea what to do.

She briefly wondered what this had to do with trust.

A thought occurred to her. Minnie took the footrest from her wheelchair. She stretched her arm out and dropped it. It landed on an invisible floor. A twisted grin formed on her face as she suddenly realized what the challenge was. She had to trust that the barrier was there.

Clever.

So why was there a staircase?

Of course!

Minnie realized that the staircase was there in case someone fell. They could simply walk up the steps and try again. Of course, Minnie wasn't able to do that.

She swallowed.

This was going to be difficult.

She ultimately wheeled onto the invisible floor. It was able to hold her weight and she sighed with relief. She then used her foot to feel in front of her. It was solid. Minnie wheeled forward and repeated the process. Her foot hit nothing. She immediately began to panic. At long last, she carefully turned and used her foot to feel the air next to her. She hit the invisible floor.

This was *very* clever.

Minnie slowly and carefully made her way across the chasm. More than once, she thought that she was going to plummet. The floor abruptly changed directions in order to throw people off. This was definitely a challenge of trust, as well as one of patience.

Minnie was shocked see that a large chunk of the floor was a straight-shot. She quickened her pace as she wheeled forward. She was so close to the other cliff!

Her foot hit air!

Minnie slammed on her brakes.

It was a clever trick. She could easily see someone running down the straight-shot and falling right off. They might be able to land on the edge of the cliff but it would be close.

Minnie turned sideways and felt solid ground beneath her foot. She inched her way around the hole and finally made it to the cliff. Her chest was rapidly rising and falling.

She pulled herself together and wheeled beneath the exit sign.

Minnie could see the door ahead.

She was going to make it!

Her heart was racing as she wheeled forward.

"HELP!"

Minnie spun around at the shriek.

She apprehensively wheeled back to the chasm.

Her heart did a somersault.

Felix was hanging from the edge of the cliff.

"Felix!" Minnie gasped, "What...?"

"I kept on running," Felix grunted.

He slipped and clawed at the rocky surface. He was eventually able to grab hold of the edge though there was no telling how long he could hold on.

"Minerva," Felix wheezed, "Help!"

Minnie gave a start and cried, "You want *me* to help *you*?"

"A very good observation of the situation," Felix snarled, "Help me!"

"Why don't you just fly?" Minnie questioned, "Or morph into something with wings?"

"It would count as magic," Felix retorted, "I can't

cheat. Arthur would—"

"Forget about Arthur!" Minnie exclaimed.

Felix looked horrified.

Sweat was rolling down his face as he continued to slip.

"Help me," Felix pleaded.

Minnie sighed and slid down from her wheelchair. She grabbed onto Felix and heaved. It took every ounce of strength that she had. Unfortunately, Felix only moved a few inches.

"I can't believe it," Felix whispered, "You're actually helping me?"

"Yeah," Minnie muttered.

"Why?"

"Because I want to be a member of the Brotherhood," Minnie quietly said, "And you know the motto. We fight together—"

"—we fall together!"

Without warning, Felix lurched backwards. Minnie screamed as he dragged her forwards. Before she knew what was happening, she found herself falling off of the cliff. It seemed to take her ages to fall. She finally hit the cold, unforgiving, ground. The wind was immediately knocked out of her. The world was nothing more than a sickening, twirling, blur. She could hear Felix chortle. It was only then that Minnie realized what had happened.

"No," Minnie grunted, "No!"

She slowly sat up.

Her world was fading the edges.

It continued to tilt and twist.

She dazedly watched as Felix staggered to his feet.

He bent over her and hissed two words:

"You're trapped."

CHAPTER SIXTEEN

Minnie's heart was thundering.

She did a quick assessment of her injuries.

The wind had been knocked out of her but her ribs still felt in-tact. She had multiple bruises and cuts but no sprains, fractures, or breaks. She realized that she was incredibly lucky.

The feeling of prosperity quickly diminished as Felix cackled.

"You're trapped, Minerva Banks," Felix taunted, "I suppose that they'll eventually come to remove your body. Yet it will be cold and rotten."

Minnie wasn't able to repress a shiver.

This only increased Felix's amusement.

It took every bit of strength that she had to keep her voice even.

"You're trapped as well," Minnie pointed out.

"Am I?"

Minnie's heart sank as she realized her mistake.

Felix's smirk deepened as he merely walked over to the staircase.

"Au revoir, Minerva Banks," Felix called, "You shan't be missed."

He began to calmly walk up the stairs.

"FELIX!" Minnie screamed, "FELIX!"

She continued to shriek until her throat was raw.

Felix ignored her as he inched his way across the invisible pathway. He eventually made it to the other side and was eaten by the darkness.

Minnie was alone.

She continued to shout his name. When it became clear that he wasn't returning, she bellowed for help. She didn't care if the help came from Arthur at this point. She just needed someone, anyone, to save her. Yet nobody came. Minnie wasn't about to give up. Her screams came from the pit of her stomach. They shook her entire body. Or perhaps it was fear that shook her body. Either way, she was trembling like a leaf caught in the wind. Minnie drew her battered knees to her chest. Her eyes and throat stung. She fought the tears but they came all the same.

Minnie broke down and began to weep.

Her body continued to violently shake. Her sobs echoed throughout the chamber. They came from a part of her that she hadn't been aware of.

The world ultimately faded away.

She was pulled in and out of consciousness.

Her body had been seriously impacted by the fall.

Minnie didn't know how much time had passed.

Minutes?

Hours?

Days?

It was all the same.

Not that it mattered anymore.

Nothing really mattered anymore.

"Your strategy doesn't seem to be working."

Minnie glanced up.

A man was sitting in front of her. His face was mostly covered by a silver river of hair; the parts that Minnie could see were lined with years of wisdom and experience. The color of his skin matched Minnie's down to the precise hue. The color of his eyes was constantly changing. A crooked hat sat atop his head. He was wearing a magnificent set of robes, upon which sat a golden 'M' pin.

Minnie swallowed before croaking, "Hey, Merlin."

"Hello, Minerva," Merlin gently said.

"Am I dead?" Minnie asked.

Her question was calm and precise.

"No," Merlin replied, "You're just a bit lost."

"I'm not lost," Minnie retorted, "I'm stuck."

It occurred to her that she probably shouldn't be talking to a sorcerer who had died sixteen-hundred-years-ago.

"Why are you here?" Minnie blurted out, "*How* are you here?"

"It appears that it's my destiny to do so."

She raised her eyebrows and asked, "Really? Destiny? That's what you're going with?"

"That's what I'm going with."

"It's your destiny to help a weeping college student?" Minnie skeptically asked.

She ran her arm across her eyes.

Merlin smiled and said, "It is my destiny to guide lost souls."

Minnie could only stare at him.

"Yes?"

"Nothing," Minnie muttered, "I can just see where the Flamels got their ability to make pretentious speeches."

A tender smile spread across Merlin's face at the mention of the Flamels.

At long last, he said, "Your strategy doesn't seem to be working."

"What strategy?" Minnie cried.

"Precisely," Merlin remarked, "You'll never get to the top at this rate."

"I can't get to the top," Minnie whispered.

"Well, not at this rate."

She miserably wiped her eyes.

"Why can't you get to the top?"

"I can't walk."

"Bummer."

Minnie let out an ugly snort.

She wiped her eyes once more and was relieved when they stayed dry.

"I would carry you," Merlin offered, "But I'm an

intangible being."

"That does put a damper on things," Minnie admitted.

"Indeed."

Minnie's sigh rattled her bones.

"There's no one around to help you," Merlin softly said.

"Thanks," Minnie bit, "I figured that one out."

"The only one who can help you is yourself."

Minnie buried her face in her hands.

"What do you want me to do?" Minnie grunted, "Spontaneously learn how to fly?"

Merlin chuckled before saying, "Thirteen steps. It'll be tough but you *can* do it."

Minnie looked up, if only to stare at him in wonder.

"I suggest that you hurry," Merlin added, "There isn't a bathroom down here."

Minnie swallowed and stammered, "I...I can't."

"Sure, you can."

Minnie resisted rolling her eyes.

She wasn't about to argue with the greatest sorcerer in history - even if he was completely wrong.

"Minerva," Merlin quietly said, "You can do this."

Minnie shivered.

Her eyes were wet once more.

"How?" Minnie finally asked.

Merlin was quiet for a moment.

At long last, he whispered, "Open your mind to the possibilities."

He stood up and began to walk away.

"W...wait!" Minnie cried, "What do I do?"

"Fight."

Minnie blinked.

He was gone.

Yet his final word echoed throughout her mind. A comforting warmth spread throughout her entire body. She lifted her chin and faced the staircase.

Minnie fought the pain as she crawled over to it.

Thirteen steps.

One.

Minnie's arms dug into the stone. She clenched her fists and gritted her teeth as she pulled herself up. It took every ounce of strength that she had.

"Give it up," Felix snarled, "You're nothing more than a pathetic retard. There's no way that you're going to get to the top."

Two.

White hot pain touched every inch of her body.

"You will never be a member of the Brotherhood of Merlin," Arthur thundered, "Never!"

Three.

Minnie was dripping with sweat.

Her chest ached as it rapidly rose and fell.

"How does it feel?" Theodore taunted, "To not

be in control of the situation?"

Four.

Her body trembled as pain and exhaustion teamed up to attack her.

"You're weak," Thomas spat.

Five.

Minnie ultimately collapsed.

For a moment, she thought that she was going to be sick.

Christopher cackled and said, "You will crumble to ash."

"Yeah," Minnie admitted, "Maybe I will."

She took a deep breath and added, "But I'll rise from those ashes."

Six.

Minnie was feeling different.

The pain was still there.

As were the nausea and exhaustion.

Yet they were drowning in waves of determination.

"Minnie," Lizzie whispered, "You can't do this."

"Yes," Minnie simply said, "I can."

Seven.

She had passed the halfway point!

"Big whoop!" Gabby teased, "Don't stop until you reach the endpoint!"

Minnie let out a shaky laugh.

Eight.

"Keep going," Miss Kiss whispered, "You're nearly there."

Nine.

"Come on, Minnie," Dmitri cried, "Don't give up!"

She wasn't planning on it.

Ten.

"I knew that you had the potential to do something great," Perry warmly said.

Eleven.

Nicolas grinned and said, "Felix is going to be pissed."

Minnie threw her head back and laughed.

Twelve.

Victor was positively glowing with pride.

What he whispered gave Minnie enough strength to reach the last step. She pulled herself to the top before promptly collapsing.

"You see," Merlin proudly said, "I knew that you could do it."

"Thanks, Merlin."

She was too tired to say anything else.

"You're welcome," Merlin replied, "Oh, can you do me a favor?"

Minnie weakly nodded.

"Look after Victor for me?"

Minnie nodded again.

It was a few moments before she had the

strength to go on. She carefully crawled across the invisible barrier. She was not about to make the wrong turn and fall back down. As amazing as her triumph had been, she wasn't about to repeat it.

Minnie finally reached the other side.

She pulled herself up into her wheelchair.

Only then did she allow herself to freak out.

She threw her head back and cheered. She pumped her fist in the air and wiped tears of joy from her eyes. She couldn't remember a time when she had been so happy.

Minnie finally pulled herself together and wheeled on.

She burst through the door.

"MINERVA!"

Something heavy slammed into her.

Minnie screamed as her wheelchair tipped backwards. She crashed to the ground with the heavy object still on top of her. Fortunately, the handles of her wheelchair separated the back of her head from the cold stone floor.

A chorus of laughter filled the room.

"Sorry."

The muffled grunt allowed Minnie to put two-and-two together.

Victor had raced across the room with the intent of hugging her. Unfortunately, he had picked up too much speed and consequences had ensued. Victor awkwardly stood up and pulled Minnie's chair back to the right position. He repeated his apology.

Minnie didn't answer; she was too busy laughing alongside the others.

"I don't care if we live for ten thousand years," Perry cackled, "I am *never* going to let you forget this."

"Thanks, Perenelle," Victor muttered.

"You're welcome."

Victor turned back to Minnie and croaked, "You're alive."

She confusedly nodded.

Nicolas stepped forward and whispered, "Felix told us that you had died."

Minnie raised an eyebrow and glanced at the vile man.

"It appears that I was mistaken," Felix meekly said.

"What happened?" Perry demanded, "I tried reading Felix's mind but he's getting too good at shielding it."

Minnie merely shook her head.

She was too shaken to speak.

Perry's hands flew to her mouth.

She eventually raised her arms.

Everyone began to gasp and cry out. It took Minnie a moment to realize that Perry had read her mind and was now sharing the memory of Felix's lowest moment.

The air immediately began to crackle and pop.

Minnie warily stared at Victor.

His fists were clenched and his mouth was twitching.

His eyes were focused on nothing.

"Victor," Nicolas slowly said, "Are you—?"

He wasn't.

He lunged forward and promptly tackled his brother. The Brotherhood flinched as Victor's fist collided with Felix's nose. Nicolas struggled to pull the two apart. Minnie had the slight feeling that he wasn't struggling as much as he could have been. Victor was able to get several more blows in before Nicolas finally restrained him.

"Victor, it's alright!" Minnie exclaimed, "I'm alright!"

"Yeah, I know," Victor gasped, "But—"

He paused.

"Hang on," Victor cried, "*How* are you alright?"

Minnie flushed.

A sniff caused her to turn.

Perry was staring at her with tears in her eyes.

"Minnie," Perry whispered, "You have to let me show them."

"No," Minnie hastily said.

"I'll make it abridged," Perry promised.

Minnie's stomach still twisted.

"They need to see it," Perry insisted, "Trust me."

Minnie hesitated before begrudgingly nodded.

Perry raised her arms once more.

Minnie closed her eyes and watched as she crawled up the steps. Perry had been kind enough to cut out the parts where she had pretended that they were all there. Minnie still awkwardly squirmed. The memory made her pain and exhaustion quite apparent.

She opened her eyes and realized that Victor was giving her a very strange look.

For a moment, Minnie wondered if Perry had shown him everything.

'No; I promise.'

Perry's words echoed throughout her mind.

Minnie sighed with relief but was still confused by Victor's demeanor.

Her confusion only escalated as Nicolas carefully released his brother. Victor stepped forward before kneeling down in front of Minnie so that the two were eye-level. Minnie was shocked to see that his eyes were wet. Without further ado, he pulled her into a warm hug.

"I'm so proud of you," Victor whispered.

Minnie's shock melted away. She ultimately returned the hug. The golden light swirled around them. Nicolas and Perry eventually joined in. It wasn't long before a majority of the Brotherhood was grouped around her. Minnie buried her face into Victor's shoulder.

She was eventually able to rasp a thank you.

The group hug eventually disbanded.

Everyone turned to glare at Felix. Minnie was amused to see that he had ducked behind a rather flustered Arthur. The other members of The Quartet were squirming with discomfort.

"Well, Arthur?" Nicolas quietly said, "You know the penalty for one member of the Brotherhood intentionally causing another one harm."

Arthur swallowed.

"Minerva's not a member of the Brotherhood," Arthur eventually said, "So—"

He was met by a chorus of boos and groans.

He gave a genuine start.

"She's proven herself," Miss Kiss exclaimed, "Let her join!"

"Let her join," Dmitri chanted, "Let her join!"

Other members of the Brotherhood picked up on it.

Minnie's face burned as several dozen voices rose up.

"Let her join," Perry pressed.

"Let her join," Nicolas commanded.

"Let her join," Victor passionately said.

"Let's put it to a vote!" Dmitri called, "All those in favor of letting her join?"

A majority of the hands went up.

Nicolas' mouth curved into a smirk as he said, "Majority rules."

Arthur looked as though Nicolas had promptly beaten him with a baseball bat.

The Brotherhood anxiously awaited their king's decision.

"Victor," Arthur abruptly said, "I'm going to let you decide."

"Decide what?" Victor asked.

"Minerva's fate is in your hands," Arthur explained, "You can either reject her from the Brotherhood of Merlin or you can make her an official member."

He held out the golden pin.

"Why would I reject her?" Victor laughed, "Of course I want her to—"

"Choose wisely," Arthur interjected, "For there is a catch."

"Of course there is," Victor muttered.

Minnie nervously swallowed.

"You can make Minerva an official member," Arthur quietly said, "Or you can move back in."

Victor blinked and whispered, "Move back in here?"

Arthur nodded.

Nicolas and Perry nervously held onto another.

Minnie's shoulders sagged. Victor had spent the

entire week talking about just how much this castle meant to him and how much he missed it. There was no doubt in Minnie's mind that he would choose Tintagel. Minnie knew that it was the right choice. It still didn't stop it from hurting. She opened her mouth to let Victor know that it was alright.

Victor's words drowned out her own.

"What?" Victor jokingly said, "And have you jerks as my roommates?"

Several people chuckled.

Nicolas and Perry both sighed with relief.

Minnie's heart skipped a beat as Victor snatched the pin from Arthur's hand. He smiled from ear-to-ear as he pinned it to her shirt.

"Who says that I want to join a group of these jerks?" Minnie teased.

Victor smirked and said, "Aw, come on. We're not all jerks."

Minnie smiled and whispered, "Thanks, Victor."

She then looked past his shoulder and called, "Hey, R, so long as we're kicking people out in order to get a room in a castle, can I kick you out?"

Victor, Perry, and Nicolas laughed.

Arthur merely scowled.

"Minerva Banks," Victor proudly said, "Welcome to the Brotherhood of Merlin."

EPILOGUE

Minnie promptly decided that this was the greatest day of her life.

Not only was she an official member of the Brotherhood of Merlin, Felix had been stripped of his points. This put him in last place which meant that he was going to lose his membership! These were the decided punishments for his actions of intending to kill Minnie. She personally thought that an eye-for-an-eye would have sufficed but she accepted this.

The Brotherhood was kneeling in the large chamber.

Arthur was sitting on his throne.

Felix was kneeling in front of him.

Arthur stared at him like one stares at a piece of garbage.

"Felix Flamel," Arthur thundered, "You knowingly and willingly tried to kill a member of the Brotherhood of Merlin. The henceforth consequence shall be exile."

Felix stared at the floor.

Minnie felt a twinge of glee.

Just a twinge.

As excited as she was, something was buzzing at the back of her mind.

She turned to the others.

Victor and Perry looked utterly delighted.

Nicolas, on the other hand, was completely stone-faced.

He was also staring right at her.

"What?" Minnie demanded.

Nicolas didn't say anything.

"This is what you wanted," Minnie pointed out, "A non-violent way to take down Felix."

"Mm."

"And you're right," Minnie continued, "It is pretty empowering."

"Is it?"

Minnie raised an eyebrow.

At long last, she said, "Yes, it is."

"Is it?"

Minnie was beginning to feel irritated.

"It's empowering," Minnie promised, "It's extremely empowering."

"Is it?"

Minnie exasperatedly threw her hands into the air.

Fortunately, she wasn't the only confused one.

"What are you getting at?" Victor asked, "Oh pretentious brother of mine?"

Perry merely stared at her husband.

"There's a difference between revenge and justice," Nicolas quietly said, "Revenge may bring a person to their knees but it will do little to help the person seeking it. Justice, on the other hand, brings down the damned and lifts up the person seeking it."

Minnie was too tired to follow along.

Nicolas sympathetically smiled and said, "In the great scheme of things, how does my brother's exile affect you?"

Minnie opened her mouth before closing it. A few seconds ago, she had felt gleeful and empowered. She now realized that Nicolas had a point. Felix would still continue being a corrupted asshole in the future. He would still feverishly fight them. He would still make her life a living hell. He would just be short a golden pin.

"What should I do?" Minnie questioned.

Nicolas leaned over and whispered, "Open your mind to the possibilities."

Minnie's eyes widened as she realized what he was getting at.

She wheeled forward and screamed, "STOP!"

All eyes turned to her.

"Felix didn't try to kill me," Minnie declared, "Forget everything that you've heard or seen. He didn't try to kill me."

The room was immediately filled with shocked whispers.

Even Felix looked taken aback.

"Minerva," Victor cried, "This is your chance to get him out."

"He never tried to kill me," Minnie firmly said.

Victor groaned.

He only brightened when he saw that Nicolas was smiling.

Minnie was also smiling.

Great minds thought alike.

And Minnie and Nicolas had just thought of the perfect plan.

A few minutes later, the Flamels and Minnie were in a side-chamber. Nicolas and Victor were holding onto their brother's arms. Felix squirmed but could not escape. Minnie sat in front of him with a large smirk on her face.

"What do you want?" Felix demanded.

"I had every intention of saving your life," Minnie pointed out, "And then I spoke up and saved your position in the Brotherhood."

"What do you want from me?" Felix snapped, "A medal?"

"According to Perry," Minnie quietly said, "A debt is made whenever one member of the Brotherhood saves another. That means that you owe me two things."

Felix's eyes widened.

Minnie threw him the vilest smirk that she could muster.

Felix bared his teeth but couldn't refuse.

It was with the utmost disdain that he growled,

"What do you want?"

"In order to make up for ensuring that you remain in the Brotherhood," Minnie thundered, "You're going to leave New Quartz University alone. You're not going to interfere with the campus. You're not going to interfere with the academic progress of any of the students, including myself. We've worked way too hard to let a self-entitled pest like you get in our way."

"Fine," Felix reluctantly replied.

"Now for the matter of me intending to save your life," Minnie continued, "You're going to do the same."

"I didn't realize that you were dying," Felix sarcastically said.

"Oh, I'm not," Minnie agreed, "Not now."

She wheeled forward and said, "You're going to save my life one day in the future. I don't know what that day's going to be. What I *do* know is that I'm constantly risking my life just by hanging out with your brother. And one day, you're going to save it."

Felix had no choice.

He ultimately stuck out his hand.

Minnie's smirk deepened as she shook it.

"Like a boss," Victor amusedly said.

"Shut up," Minnie laughed.

The group entered the main chamber once more.

"Ah," Arthur boomed, "You're just in time."

"In time for what?" Minnie warily asked.

"For our last challenge!"

They exchanged glances.

"Minerva's already a member of the Brotherhood," Victor spoke up.

"How conceited," Arthur snapped, "Thinking that you two are the only reasons that we're doing this examination. It has been a tradition for centuries. As has the last challenge."

"What's the last challenge?" Minnie questioned.

She was expecting some sort of torturous obstacle.

As such, she was taken aback when Arthur turned to a member of the Brotherhood and asked, "What do you stand for?"

The man hesitated before saying, "I stand for my family."

Arthur turned to a second member and repeated the question.

"I stand for justice."

One by one, people gave their answers:

"I stand for integrity."

"I stand for love."

"I stand for life."

Nicolas and Perry both stood for peace and equality.

Dmitri stood for his friends.

Miss Kiss stood for those who could not stand for themselves.

"Well, Minerva Banks?" Arthur demanded, "What do you stand for?"

"I don't stand for anything," Minnie shot back.

"Do you mean that you are neutral?"

Minnie grinned and said, "No - I'm still calling myself an Antagonist."

"So, what do you stand for?"

"I don't stand for anything."

He frowned before saying, "Do you mean that you don't have anything to stand for?"

"No," Minnie cried, "I mean that I don't stand for anything. I *can't* stand for anything!"

"Why not?"

"Because I can't stand at all!"

A deafening silence filled the room.

It was interrupted by an ugly snort, courtesy of Victor.

It wasn't long before nearly everyone was laughing.

"ENOUGH!"

Arthur's roar shook the windows but it was still a few moments before the laughter completely died. He looked furious. Minnie triumphantly smiled. Perhaps she had gotten to the Brotherhood after all.

"Victor," Arthur spat, "What do *you* stand for?"

"Merlin," Victor immediately said.

Whispers of approval rang throughout the room.

"Oh, you do?" Arthur mockingly said, "You stand for Merlin? Well, isn't that nice. So do you stand for the Merlin who tried to stop you from talking to Nimue? Do you stand for the Merlin who was put under her spell because of you? Do you stand for the Merlin who was dragged beneath the lake because of you?"

Victor raised an eyebrow.

"I stand for the Merlin who believed in peace and equality," Victor quietly said, "I stand for the Merlin who found three shivering boys in a tree and took them in. I stand for the Merlin who took in other children until he had created a family - a Brotherhood."

His voice had risen.

It shook with passion as he continued, "I stand for the Merlin who taught us into the early hours of the morning. I stand for the Merlin who comforted us when we were scared. I stand for the Merlin who had the nerve to ground me just for putting honey in Nicolas' hair."

Nearly everyone giggled.

"I stand for the Merlin who treated us like we were his equals," Victor went on, "I stand for the Merlin who could see into the future. I stand for the Merlin who said that it was possible to love everyone and anyone, regardless of their gender, appearance, race, ability..."

He broke off for a moment before reverently continuing, "I stand for the Merlin who told us that mistakes were like the phoenix - we may crumble to ash but we would rise from those ashes. I stand for the Merlin who gave us our tattoos. I stand for the Merlin who gave us our golden pins. I stand for the Merlin who told us to open our minds to the possibilities. I stand for the Merlin who inspired us. I stand for the Merlin who respected us. I stand for the Merlin who loved us. I stand for Merlin!"

He was shaking.

The air was crackling.

Minnie began to clap, as did many others.

"Stop!" Arthur snapped, "I don't want to hear a single sound!"

Minnie raised her eyebrows.

She slowly lifted her hands into the air until they were on either side of her head. She then began to rapidly shake them. The others stared at her. Perry eventually smiled before mimicking her movements. The other members of the Brotherhood followed suit.

Arthur's eye began to twitch.

Minnie threw him a smirk.

"You really think that you can best me?" Arthur hissed.

"Yeah."

"I am Arthur," Arthur boomed, "I am one of the

most powerful sorcerers to have ever existed! I am the King of the Brotherhood of Merlin! I am the wielder of Excalibur! Surely you don't believe that you could possibly defeat me?"

He towered over Minnie as he spat, "You are a mere mortal! A disabled one at that! You are pathetic! You are useless! You are nothing! You are-"

Yet exactly what Minnie was would remain unsaid.

For at that moment, her fist promptly collided with Arthur's jaw.

The sickening crack was drowned out by the chorus of gasps. Arthur staggered backwards and ended up tripping over his own cloak. He fell onto his back where he lay in a piteous heap.

Minnie clutched her throbbing fist.

She was just as stunned as the others.

At long last, she muttered, "Huh..."

It took a quarter of an hour for her to fully register what she had done and what it meant. Arthur hadn't been seriously hurt. His pride was wounded more than anything else. But such an injury was still notable.

Victor was positively gushing.

"The look on his face when he slunk out of the chamber," Victor chortled, "I have never seen him look so taken aback!"

Nicolas smiled as he finished wrapping Minnie's

hand. Perry handed her a vial and she appreciatively drank the contents.

"You're going to have some swelling," Perry noted, "Let me know if it doesn't go down within the hour."

Minnie nodded.

She gazed at her bandaged hand, still awestruck by what she had done.

"Sorry, Nicolas," Minnie finally said, "I know that you're a pacifist."

Nicolas nodded and said, "Yes, I am."

He hesitated before adding, "However, as Merlin said, it's important to open your mind to the possibilities!"

The four laughed as they began to pack.

Nicolas and Victor ducked into one room to clean up, leaving Minnie and Perry to the other room. They shoved everything into the bags as they talked about the long week.

"I think that that's everything," Minnie eventually said.

"Can you go see how the boys are doing?" Perry asked.

Minnie nodded and went to wheel next door.

She paused when she realized that Victor and Nicolas were talking.

"You're never going to be able to prove that Kellington is—"

"I know, I know."

"It doesn't even make sense."

"I know but—"

"But what?"

"I overheard him talking the other day."

"And?"

"He said something about necromancy."

"What?"

"Mmhm."

"You're joking?"

"I wish."

There was a pause.

Then:

"I'm way too tired to deal with this right now."

Victor chuckled and said, "As am I."

Minnie was about to knock on the door.

"So," Victor carefully said, "What do you think of Minerva?"

Minnie's eyes widened.

She could hear Nicolas chuckle.

"What?" Victor snapped.

"Where did that come from?" Nicolas cried.

Minnie could envision Victor shrugging.

There was a suspenseful moment of silence.

"So," Victor prompted, "What do you think?"

Minnie could tell that Nicolas was smiling.

"I think," Nicolas gently said, "You'd better learn how to swim."

Minnie's cheeks were on fire.

"Are you worried about her?" Nicolas wondered.

"I'm always worried about her," Victor teased.

He had said the same thing a few nights ago.

Nicolas made a thoughtful noise.

"What?"

"Nothing," Nicolas replied, "It's just..."

"Just what?"

"If you're always worrying about her," Nicolas thoughtfully said, "Who's going to worry about you?"

Minnie opened the door and said, "I am."

Victor smiled and Minnie returned it.

Nicolas hid his own smile.

The three looked up as Dmitri raced into the room.

His face was red and pinched.

"What's wrong?" Victor immediately asked.

"Arthur's going to kick me out of the Brotherhood," Dmitri gasped.

"The hell he is!"

The Flamels and Minnie gathered their things before following Dmitri down to the entrance hall. A smirking Arthur was waiting for them.

"It was very generous of you to spare Felix's position, Minerva," Arthur slyly said, "That puts Dmitri in last place which means that he's going to be removed."

"No," Victor quietly said, "He's not."

Arthur ignored him.

He went to grab the pin from Dmitri's shirt.

Minnie hastily tapped her scabbard and withdrew her sword.

There was no need.

A strange invisible wall slammed into Arthur. It sent him flying into the wall. The air crackled and popped. Minnie glanced at Nicolas before realizing that he was passively smiling.

Victor, on the other hand, was lowering his hands.

His eyes were lit up with the typical fire.

Minnie felt a rush of pride and affection.

"You did it!" Dmitri exclaimed, "You did The Push!"

Victor puffed out his chest before walking over to the fallen Arthur. Minnie was right at his side. Arthur quickly withdrew Excalibur. Minnie used her own sword to deflect the blade. She grabbed the king's wrist and twisted, as Victor had shown her. The sword ultimately fell to the ground. Victor sent out another wave of energy that knocked it across the hall.

"You really think that we're Antagonists?" Victor coldly said, "You really think that we're going to cause the Brotherhood to crumble?"

He bent down and said, "Then I suggest that you don't cross us."

"You're threatening me?" Arthur gasped.

"Yes," Minnie declared, "We are."

"Do you know what's funny, R?" Victor asked, "You were faced with your own challenge this week. You thought that it would be easy - beating and berating us until we were nothing more than a pile of ash."

"You never expected us to rise from the ashes," Minnie added.

"Only, we did," Victor triumphantly said.

"And now," Minnie cried, "We're stronger than ever before."

Victor nodded and said, "And we *will not hesitate* to bring you down."

Arthur winced.

"Dmitri stays," Victor finished, "Or else."

Arthur went to stand up but Victor knocked him down once more.

"What happens if I just kick you out of the Brotherhood?" Arthur snarled.

Nicolas stepped forward and said, "I take the crown and the sword, henceforth becoming the true King of the Brotherhood of Merlin."

Arthur was trapped.

He glared up at them before growling, "Get out of my castle."

"Your castle?" Victor repeated, "*Your* castle? This isn't your castle, R. This castle belongs to the

Brotherhood of Merlin. It's our home. It's *my* home and no matter what you say, no matter what you try to do, I will *always* come home."

He turned to the others before saying, "However, at the moment, I think that we really ought to leave."

The others nodded in agreement.

Nicolas spoke up, "Do you still want to...?"

"Of course," Victor cried, "It's traditional.

"Are you going to go look at that stupid tree?"

They glanced down at Arthur.

Nicolas and Victor exchanged solemn looks.

"Hey," Victor eventually said, "We can't help it if we weren't all born with silver spoons sticking out of our mouths."

"Victor," Nicolas chastised, "Don't insult him. He was not born with a silver spoon sticking out of his mouth. He was born with a *golden* spoon sticking out of his mouth."

Victor smiled.

It faded away as another man entered the entrance hall.

"Ah, Felix," Arthur boomed, "The Knights and I have dinner reservations at a five-star restaurant in the heart of London. Shall you join us?"

"It would be an honor, Your Highness," Felix replied, "Thank you for the invitation."

Minnie resisted rolling her eyes.

"Excellent," Arthur cheerfully said, "We best be on our w—"

"Unfortunately," Felix continued, "I can't."

"Excuse me?"

"I can't, Your Highness," Felix apologetically said, "I'm afraid that I have to do something else at the moment."

"What do you have to do?"

Felix smirked and said, "I have to go look at that stupid tree."

Arthur frowned as his own words were thrown back at him.

The King of the Brotherhood of Merlin ultimately slunked away.

The brothers exchanged glances but didn't say a word.

They continued to remain silent as they made their way through the castle and out onto the grounds. Minnie and Perry followed. Miss Kiss and Dmitri eventually joined them as well.

"God damn," Miss Kiss eventually said.

Dmitri giggled and Victor glared at her.

"Sorry," Miss Kiss apologized, "But really...that was...damn..."

Victor chuckled.

"Stuff like that makes me really glad that you two aren't supervillains," Miss Kiss muttered, "New Quartz City wouldn't stand a chance."

"You flatter us," Victor simply said.

"I suppose that that's a perk of being an Antagonist," Miss Kiss continued, "Getting to act evil when you want to."

"Actually, you're not that far off," Victor admitted, "It's more about not having to care about what other people think. Don't get me wrong - I try to help as many people as I can and it hurts when you genuinely make a mistake that you can't take back."

His eyes flickered over to the lake before he continued, "Then again, when everyone's calling you an Antagonist, it allows you to get away with a lot of things."

She laughed.

"No, really," Victor cried.

He clapped Felix on the shoulder before saying, "Look at Felix. Whenever he's at New Quartz City, he's under a microscope. He pretends to fight evil, he gives out fancy speeches, he makes large donations, he throws friends under the bus...he does whatever he can so that people think that he's the good guy. All it takes is one wrong slip and he's done."

"That's pretty much how my entire worldview changed," Minnie admitted.

"Whereas I can do whatever I want," Victor continued, "Break into a hospital? No problem! Impersonate someone in order to steal their bank statements? Done! Crash through the wall of a lecture hall? Why not? I'm an Antagonist."

"True," Felix coolly said, "The difference is that you can never be rewarded for the good that you try to do because everyone thinks that you're a supervillain."

Victor pointed to his heart and mockingly said, "The award is in here, dear brother."

"Keep telling yourself that," Felix shot back, "But sooner or later you're going to realize that one's reputation can be a very powerful thing."

"We're here," Nicolas abruptly said.

Minnie nearly crashed into Victor as the crowd came to a screeching halt.

Minnie found herself staring at an enormous tree. The trunk was twisted and there was a large burrow beneath. Other than that, it was nothing out of the ordinary.

And yet, Victor, Nicolas, and Felix were all smiling at it.

They stepped forward.

Perry, Miss Kiss, Dmitri, and Minnie hung back.

The latter was extremely confused.

Perry chuckled before raising her hand.

Minnie gasped as several images appeared in her mind. It was like she was watching a movie.

Three boys were squashed together in the burrow of the tree.

A teenager with bright blue eyes.

A preteen with golden eyes.

A small child with purple eyes.

The child and the preteen were climbing the branches as the teenager anxiously watched.

The three boys were sitting on one of the branches.

They were gazing at the stars.

A storm arose.

The three boys huddled in the burrow, holding onto one another, praying...

And then a man was there...

He spoke to them with kind words.

He was smiling as he held out his hand.

He invited them to come live in the castle.

He invited them to join his Brotherhood...

Minnie wiped tears from her eyes.

She had no idea what to say.

In the end, nobody said anything.

The group finally turned around and made their way back to the castle.

Felix gave his brothers a pat on the shoulder before ultimately leaving them.

Minnie still hated him.

She heard Perry chuckle.

"So," Dmitri sighed, "You're leaving, huh?"

"Do you want to come with us?" Victor offered.

His eyes lit up.

At long last, he muttered, "Nah. Someone has to

keep Arthur on edge."

Victor laughed before pulling him into a tight hug.

"Take care of yourself, kid," Victor murmured.

"You too."

They pulled apart.

"So," Minnie spoke up, "How exactly are we getting back to New Quartz City?"

"Well," Victor slyly said, "Dmitri and I had a long conversation the other night. He was nice enough to give me something that's very dear to me."

"What's that?"

Victor merely smirked.

He brought his fingers to his lips and whistled.

A deafening roar caused everyone to jump.

Minnie gasped as Firestone soared towards him. His wings created a breeze that tousled everyone's hair and clothes. The griffin gracefully landed next to Victor. The sixteen-hundred-year-old sorcerer affectionately petted him. Minnie realized that Firestone was now proudly bearing a gigantic saddle complete with saddlebags that were the size of Minnie.

She could only laugh with amazement.

They had a pet griffin!

"I'm not changing his litter box," Minnie finally said.

Victor roared with laughter.

He helped Minnie onto the saddle, folded up the wheelchair, and placed it into one of the saddlebags. He then climbed onto Firestone's head.

He grinned down at his brother and sister-in-law.

"Can we drop you anywhere?" Victor called.

Nicolas chuckled before mumbling, "Oh, what the heck?"

"I call shotgun," Perry exclaimed.

The two climbed up onto the griffin. Perry plopped next to Victor and Nicolas gracefully sat down next to Minnie. Victor gave the command and Firestone rose into the air. Dmitri and Miss Kiss waved and shouted goodbye. Minnie realized that she was really going to miss them.

"So," Minnie finally said, "Where exactly are we going to keep Firestone?"

"Don't worry about it," Victor chuckled.

"I sort of think that I should?"

"Merlin used to say that one should not prioritize on the destination," Nicolas pointed out, "Rather, they should focus on the journey."

"Merlin said that?"

Nicolas nodded.

"Huh," Minnie muttered, "Well, if nothing else, at least his legacy lives on through those papers that are folded up inside the fortune cookies."

She reached over the saddle's lip and stroked

Firestone's mixture of fur and feathers.

A thought struck her.

"Can I ride Firestone to New Quartz University?" Minnie playfully asked.

"Sure," Victor chuckled, "Just don't lose him."

Minnie shrugged and said, "I'll tie him to a bike rack."

The others laughed as the griffin angrily huffed.

Victor glanced over his shoulder.

His smile slipped away.

He slid down into the saddle and sadly stared out towards the sky. Minnie squinted before finally realizing what he was looking at. Castle Tintagel was nothing more than a silhouette against the night sky. Several clouds rolled over and blocked their view.

It was gone.

Nicolas put a hand on his brother's shoulder and gently said, "We'll be back."

Victor nodded before softly saying, "Let's go home…"

Made in the USA
Middletown, DE
02 December 2019